I0673315

Beyond Measure 2

By: K.D. Harris

STREET KNOWLEDGE PUBLISHING

Published by: Street Knowledge Publishing

Street Knowledge Publishing
P.O. Box 345
Wilmington, DE 19899

Copyright date: 2012
ISBN: 978-1-944151-06-5

Beyond Measure 2 a novel by K. D. Harris

Edited by: Navimjan Services LLC
Cover design by: Street Knowledge Publishing Services
Formatted by:
Typed from handwriting to text by:
Female model on cover:
Male model:

www.streetknowledgepublishing.com

Printed in Canada

Chapter 1

"Happy Birthday to you...Happy Birthday to you...Happy Birthday Dear Azariaaah-Happy Birrrthday to youuuu...." Everyone sang in unison around the picnic table as Azariah beamed from all the attention she was getting.

"Make a wish," Jay whispered in her ear.

She then leaned over and blew out all seven candles on her purple and hot pink guitar shaped Hannah Montana cake. After all the candles were blown out everyone clapped their hands and cheered. Azariah batted her curly lashes and gave everyone her signature Miss America wave and nodded her head as she embraced the praise she was received. She had grown into a beautiful little girl; her Mahogany complexion, and sparkling green eyes came from my father. She was an amazing little girl; she sang in the church choir, danced with the church's praise group, and to top it off, she was an honor roll student.

"She is such a little diva." Aunt Rosa said with a chuckle.

I couldn't help but to agree. Azariah was a special case. I swore she's been here before. The things that she would say and her actions were those of a much older person. My father described it as being wise beyond her years. To me it was just creepy.

"Daddy can I have the biggest piece? She asked in a bubbly voice as she took hold of the knife.

"Hey! Wait a minute!" I panicked and hurried over to her to quickly, yet carefully, remove the knife from her grasp.
"Zariah let Mommy help you with that. Sweetie knives can be dangerous. Ok?" I explained.

Unfortunately it didn't sit well with her. She folded her arms across her chest and poked out her pink heavily glossed lips.

"I don't want it anymore!" She yelled.

Huge tears cascaded down her chunky cheeks. All eyes were on me as if I had committed a crime. Jay wrapped her in his arms to console her.

"Sasha, come on give her a break, let her cut it. I'm right here by her side. Do you think I would let my baby hurt herself?"

I reluctantly moved away and let them cut the cake. My stomach began to knot up and a lump formed in my throat. My feelings were hurt as I watched them with a tinge of jealousy.

It never failed. He always let her have what she wanted. I guess he tried extra hard since in his mind he wasn't her biological father. After they were finished he must have noticed that I was upset because he made his way over to me and wrapped his strong arms around my protruding waist. He whispered in my ear.

"Don't be so over protective with her. Remember you have two new little ones to look after now." He said as he pointed to Sarai and Jai, our six week old twins.

I glanced over at my precious bundles of joy; the heaviness I was feeling immediately lifted.

"Yeah, and let's not forget Little Jay." I reminded him and laughed lightly.

Jay shook his head sighed and laughed. Little Jay was our rambunctious four year old. He was pure entertainment. There was never a dull moment with him around. At the present time he was running around chasing my sister's eight year old son with a super soaker water gun that was practically twice his size. My dad yelled at him a few times warning him to be careful around his grill. Most little kids were afraid of my dad when he raised his deep baritone voice. Not Lil' Jay. My dad's warning had fallen on death ears. He kept doing what he did best...him.

Jay planted warm sweet kisses on my neck still trying to comfort me. I guess I may have overreacted a little by the way he treated Azariah. I should be happy because most men wouldn't take to a child that wasn't theirs. Sometimes deep in my mind I believe that Jay may have known the truth about Azariah's paternity.

Or maybe I should just tell him the truth.

As quickly as the thought would come, it would go. I would lose everything if he found out that I had lied to him all this time. Jay was a spiritual man with morals and pride. There would be no way he could forgive me for being so deceitful, especially about something like that. Sometimes I'd have the urge to come clean; but then would think about my family. I refused to lose them. I went all of my life without them. I deserved happiness after everything I went through. Thanks to the Haywards I had finally been able to witness Bliss; these last seven years have been wonderful. I was officially a Psychiatrist and had my own practice where I specialized in domestic violence and pediatric psychology. My office was connected to the Battered Woman's shelter I ran. Jay was now a partner at his firm. He had scored some major accounts, and traveled frequently, however, still managed to be home for family events, and school recitals.

I tried to forget about the people in my past. The only person I would talk to from that era was Starla. She was living with her boyfriend in Arizona. She dropped out of college her junior year and became a freelance photographer. I guess following after her father's footsteps. She had come to visit this past Christmas. I couldn't believe how much she'd grown. She looked like a light skinned Camille.

"Sasha...I think this little one is hungry." Aunt Rosa taunted, holding Jai in the air.

"He just ate not even an hour ago. My breasts are killing me!" Gently rubbing my breast to prepare them for the abuse they were about to receive.

She laughed and handed him to me. I took him in the house and sat in the rocking chair in the sitting room. I unsnapped my nursing bra and placed my nipple to his mouth. He greedily latched on.

Damn.... He's worse than his daddy.

I closed my eyes and rocked in the chair as I did my motherly duty. A few minutes later I heard my doorbell chime. I continued feeding Jai figuring someone would get it. It rang a few more times. I looked around to see if anyone was coming to answer it then sighed. I guess the dang music is too loud for them to hear. I gently removed my nipple from his mouth. He began to frown his little face up to cry.

"Oh don't cry lil' baby momma gonna be right back for her little man." I sang quietly placing the binky in his mouth and sitting him in the baby bouncer.

The door bell rang again.

"Coming...." I yelled out. I opened the door and a Fed Ex guy was standing there with a little package.

"Is there a Miss Azariah Hayward here?" he asked.

"I am her mother...."

"Could you sign here please?" He handed me a little electronic notepad. I signed and then he handed me the package.

"Have a good day ma'am." He said and turned away.

I examined the package. I was searching to see who it was from. There was nothing on the outside. I shut my door and opened the box. It was a jewelry case. I opened the case and it was a stunning diamond and platinum charm bracelet.

Wow.

One of the charms had a heart engraved 'Daddy's little girl'. Jay really out did himself this time. He always tried to do extra things for Azariah. This time he had truly outdone himself. I looked at the bracelet again. This had to cost a fortune. There was no way I could allow him to give this to her she was only seven. I went back to the den to check on Jai. He was fast asleep. I picked up the phone and dialed Jay's cell number he had a lot of explaining to do.

7

Chapter 2

I called Jay and a few minutes later he showed up in the den. I placed my arms around his neck and nibbled on his sweet spot. I had to play nice before I went in for the kill.

"Baby I need to show you something," I said in a sweet voice while planting soft kisses on his face. I could feel his manhood rising and that's where I wanted him to be. I stepped back.

"Damn baby don't stop," he moaned.

"I just wanted to let you know that you are an awesome father; Especially to Azariah. But don't you think this is a little too much for a seven year old."

I removed the bracelet from my side pocket. He took the bracelet from my hand and looked it over.

"Where did this come from?" He asked a looking confused. "I didn't buy this Sasha," he exclaimed as he handed the bracelet back to me.

I was starting to get a little irritated. I couldn't believe he would sit here and lie to me...in my face and it wasn't that serious.

"You don't have to lie Jay. This bracelet has your name written all over it. You always spoil that girl. You better stop; you're creating a monster."

"Seriously, Sash I didn't buy that bracelet. Maybe you should ask Mixxon...he spoils her as much as I do." He attempted to walk away but I stopped him.

"Whoa, wait a minute Mr. I'm not finished talking to you and my dad didn't buy this bracelet. He bought her a new bike which is something that you buy a seven year old. He doesn't even have money like that to buy things like this."

"Exactly, this has to be a worth a few thousand dollars. Use your brain Sasha, you know I wouldn't do that." He left me standing there looking stupid.

This fine piece of jewelry was definitely grown up. I sat on the couch, in a complete muddle. I looked at the bracelet again and shook my head. If he didn't buy it than who did?

***

"Mom-mee...Mom-meee!" growled little Jay. He was climbing on my bed like an animal. "I'm gonna eat you up!" he said.

I put my head under the covers to act as if I was afraid and hiding from him. "Please don't eat me Mr. *Bear*?" I asked not sure of which animal he was pretending to be this morning.

He ended his theatrics and sulked, "Mom...I'm not a bear I'm a mountain lion, you know like the kind I saw at the Baltimore Zoo with Poppi!" He said excitedly.

"Oh...ok next time I'll be prepared." I extended my arms for him to come hug me. He crawled to me and gave me a big wet kiss on the cheek. I sat on the side of the bed and began to tickle him. He looked so much like his father. He had his soft brown eyes, and a golden brown complexion. The twins favored him a lot; Sarai just looked like a female version of the boys. Not in a bad way.

When Azariah was a baby she looked like Jay but as she got older she pretty much developed her own look. My dad said she reminded him of his mother. I thanked God that she changed because I wasn't prepared for anyone to start asking questions.

I checked the time, it was 8:30a.m. I didn't expect it to be that late. I figured it to be at least 6:30a.m. because the twins didn't wake up for their feeding. I sat Lil' Jay on the floor and went to the nursery. I opened the door to find the twins weren't there. Feeling uneasy as my heartbeat increased. Jay had left the day after the party for meetings in Chicago and wouldn't be home until tomorrow evening sometime. I checked in Azariah's room she was sitting at her vanity table brushing her hair. She was so into her hair that she didn't even notice me in the room. She tried so hard to brush her soft curls out. She wanted her hair straight like her Auntie Jehaida. She even asked me to put a relaxer in it once. I explained to her that her hair would fall out and that ended her quest for a relaxer.

"Zar...umm do you know if any one's been here? I asked. She sat her brush down. "Auntie Mara came early this morning...I think she's down stairs with *your* babies." She said rudely.

She picked her brush back up and went back to brushing. I was about to say something about her attitude but I decided against it. I hurried down the stairs in search of Xiomara and the twins. Checking all the rooms I didn't see them. I heard a cry come from the basement so I went down there and found them in the pack-n-plays while Xiomara worked out.

I wanted to curse her out but was so relieved to see the kids. I picked up Sarai and held her close. She turned off the treadmill and came over to me. I rolled my eyes as she came towards me.

"Don't you ever take my kids and without telling me again!" I snapped.

Xiomara stood in front of me with a hurt look on her face.

"Damn, sis I was only trying to give you a break!" she said defensively.

She threw her towel over her shoulder and headed towards the steps. I picked Jai up and followed behind her. I felt bad about snapping like that. Once upstairs, I put the babies in their bouncers and went in the kitchen after Xiomara. She was in the fridge pouring herself a glass of vitamin water. I took a seat at the breakfast nook.

"Mara...I'm so sorry. I know you were just trying to help." I said apologetically. "But I was scared...weird things have been happening since Saturday and that just threw me off a little." I explained.

She grabbed her water and sat in front of me, "What weird things?" she asked.

I went on, explaining about the bracelet that came in the mail for Azariah and how I've been getting calls with no one speaking on the other end. She didn't seem too concerned about the calls, but she was interested in the bracelet.

"Let me see the bracelet."

I went to my office and pulled the box from my desk. I went back to the kitchen and handed her the box. She opened it and put her hand over her mouth in astonishment.

"Oh my God...this is beautiful!" she gasped.

"I know right look at the heart, it says 'Daddy's little girl'. Jay claims he didn't buy that." I said.

She continued to admire the bracelet.

"Maybe Pastor Duncan bought it for her, that is his step-granddaughter. I mean he treats her just like his own maybe he did it" she said.

I shook my head, "No...He didn't buy it either."

She put the bracelet back in the box.

"Well...I know who it didn't come from…."she said with a smirk. "Her real daddy...cause he's six feet under where his ass should be!" her whole demeanor changed.

She hated Lorenz even in death. No one besides Camille and Shelly knew the truth about Azariah's paternity. They still believed she was Lorenz's child. Chills ran through my body whenever I thought about him. Memories of his abuse would haunt me. Had to admit sometimes that I blamed myself for his madness. I thought that if I could have been just a little stronger I could have saved him. But it was too late for that now. He was gone. I changed the subject.

"So what are you doing for Mother's day?" I asked.

She took a sip out of her glass and sat it down, "Chuck and the kids are taking me to dinner and a movie she said. They want to do a family date."

"So do you have any idea what Jay and the kids have planned for you?"She asked.

"Not really. Jay is upset with me. We've been arguing off and on about the bracelet since Saturday. He didn't even tell me bye when he left. Most likely we'll just go to church and then to his parents house afterwards."

She was about to say something until we were interrupted by Lil' Jay who came running into the room; Azariah was hot on his tracks. I rolled my eyes as the drama was about to unfold. I grabbed him up and put my hand up to stop Azariah in her pursuit.

"What's going on? I asked. They both started screaming and yelling at once. "Use your indoor voices and one at a time! " I demanded, " Azariah you go first"

"Jay won't give me back my picture," she whined. I looked in Jay's hand and saw that he was holding something. I took the picture out of his hand and read the back of it and the words '*Mommy and Daddy 2007*' where written on the back of it.

I turned the picture around and it was of me and Lorenz at Caesar's Palace in Atlantic City. I dropped the picture and grabbed Azariah's arm.

"Where in the hell did you get this from!" I yelled.

She began to cry. "I found it out back yesterday. It was in an envelope and it had my name on it." I began to shake her.

"Out back...yesterday? Why didn't you tell me about this yesterday!" I was livid. I hadn't seen that picture in years. She had to be lying. She must have been in the attic going through the old pictures.

Xiomara snatched Azariah from my grip, "Sasha! What the hell are you doing? Don't touch her like that; she's a little girl for Christ sakes." She snapped.

I held the picture up for her to see it. She snatched it from me, "How did she get this?" she asked.

Azariah was now hiding behind Xiomara.

She told her the same thing she told me. I wasn't buying it.

"Zar, don't lie to me. Where you in the attic? Tell me the truth and I won't be mad." I spoke to her in a calm voice hoping that she would come clean.

"Mommy, I'm telling the truth. I found it out back." She whimpered.

I ran to the backyard and looked around. I didn't see anything suspicious; then again I probably wouldn't if it did indeed happen yesterday.

I walked back into the house. Zar was now sitting next Xiomara. She looked at me with fear in her eyes. Something she had never done. At the time I could feel no compassion. I was afraid. Something bizarre was going on and I had to get to the bottom of it fast. I went to my office and dialed Jay. The phone rang and rang. I hung up and immediately dialed again. The same thing. I repeated it several times. I felt like a young girl trying to get her cheating man to answer. Finally after the eighth time he answered.

"What!" He was annoyed but I didn't care.

"Jay...I need you home now! Someone has been on our property and I think they're stalking Azariah!" I was frantic.

"What? Why would you think that?"

I took a deep breath a repeated the scenario the she explained it to me.

He sighed heavily before he spoke, "Sasha you're over reacting. No one is stalking Zar. Are you sure you didn't save one of his pictures? Maybe you left one out by mistake. Who knows it could have gotten mixed up in your things from the move". He said nonchalantly.

I removed the phone from my ear and stared at in awe. *Was he serious? The move?*

"Did you say the move? We moved damn near seven years ago Jay! Why in HELL would I still have pictures of Lorenz surfacing around. Do you know what it said on the back of it? Mommy and Daddy! I never wrote that!" I said in aggravation. I was getting peeved. I wish I could have punched him through the phone.

"You know what Sasha? I really don't have time for this right now. We will talk when I get home Monday. To make you feel better call around and see how much it would be to add a privacy fence for the backyard, we need one anyway."

The only thing I heard was 'Not coming home until Monday'.

"Monday...you're not coming back until Monday? I said sadly. You do realize that Mother's Day is Sunday? We are always together as a family on holidays...what am I supposed to do with you not here? "

"Sash...look I have to close this deal. It's important, very important that I handle this. I'll make it up to you on Monday. Now look I have to go, I'll call and talk to the kids tomorrow. I love you." He said with empathy.

"I love you too" I responded.

He hung up the phone but I still had the phone to my ear and began to cry softly. I couldn't believe he wasn't coming home. We needed him here and he was leaving us hanging. I wiped my eyes and grabbed the phone book. Fences, I needed to find a service that could come out immediately. I called a few businesses and finally lucked up. They told me they could have someone out that afternoon to do an estimate. I didn't care how much it cost. I just wanted it up quick, fast and in a hurry.

Later that evening, I went to Azariah's room to apologize for snapping at her the way I did. I know she was afraid by my actions. I had never laid a hand on her...I didn't have to because she was a great kid. I peeked through the door and she was sitting on her bed with her netbook on her lap. She seemed heavily engrossed with whatever she was doing. I decided to knock on her door before entering.

"Zar, Can I come in? "She didn't answer she closed her screen, and tossed her computer to the side like it was nothing. I sat on the bed next to her.

She turned her head in the opposite direction away from me. I knew she was still angry from earlier. So I had to make it right. I ran my hands through her hair.

"Baby I am so sorry if I scared you earlier. I only reacted that way because of fear. I thought someone was trying to hurt you."

Azariah turned over and stared at me with a confused look. I lay down next to her and wrapped my arms around her.

"Mommy…how could a picture hurt me? It was just a picture. It had my name on it. So it was my picture."

She frowned her face up and turned her back to me.

If she only knew how much a picture could actually hurt her.

I decided to leave her alone. I didn't want her to ask any questions that I couldn't answer just yet.

Chapter 3

Service was beautiful today. The kids of the church did a presentation for all the mothers. After church, everyone went over to Mom Duncan's for the Mother's Day Dinner. I really didn't feel like going, but I went anyway. Everyone from the church was there having a good time. I took the babies in the house because it was extremely hot outside. I watched the kids through the window; they were running around having a ball. All except Zar; she was sitting by herself at the picnic table. She was doing something on her cell phone. I figured she must have been texting her little friends from school. After a few more minutes of spying, I decided it was safe for me to go and get comfortable.

I found a quiet area in the living room and called my sisters to wish them a happy mother's day. Of course no one was home. Jehaida went on a cruise and her oldest was home with the kids. I told her happy mother's day in advance. She was pregnant with her third child. She was due at the end of August, right before she starts her sophomore year in college. She already had two kids that she birthed in high school. I hung up and made a mental note to curse Jehaida out when she came home. I couldn't believe she didn't tell me she was going on a cruise. I would have gone with her if I had known I wouldn't be doing anything special.

Around six in the evening, I gathered the kids and said our goodbyes. As I was on my way out I was stopped by Mom Duncan.

"Sasha sweetie why don't you leave the children here with me?" she asked sweetly.

"Mom I can't do that. You need to rest. You've been busy cooking and entertaining guest all day."

She smiled, "Baby what is that supposed to mean. After all these years I've learned to multi tasked. Besides if I need help Sister Mills and my sweet Azariah can assist me." She winked in Zar's direction.

Zar wasn't paying attention to what was going on she was too busy texting away on her cell phone. I decided to give in. Admittedly, I would enjoy an evening to myself without the stress of children.

"Ok Mom. Let me go home and get the babies formula-" She stopped me in the middle of my sentence.

"Formula?" She wrinkled her face.

"Yes Formula. I gave up on breast feeding. It was hard enough to do it with one baby, twins were overbearing!" I laughed trying to ease the moment.

She shook her head and started to gather the babies. She was old fashioned and didn't understand that times had changed. I would be going back to work soon anyway so there was no way I could continue to provide milk for both babies. I gave the babies quick kisses before I could get to little Jay he was already gone in the wind; he loved staying at his grandparents. I went to hug Zar and she backed away.

"What's wrong with you?"

She began to pout. "Why do I need to stay here? I want to go home." She rolled her eyes and whined.

I couldn't believe it. She usually loves to be with her Mom-mom. I told her I would see her in the morning. She continued to protest. At this point everyone was staring. I had no choice but to get stern with her.

"Azariah your behavior is unacceptable. If you don't straighten up I will take your phone away." She snatched

17

herself from my grip and stomped in the house. I looked up at Mom Duncan and hurt was in her eyes. I apologized for her actions. She told me not to worry about it but I could see she was offended.

During my drive home, I couldn't get Zar off my mind. She had really become distant lately. She was really moody and shrewd with her words. I had seen this with a few children I had as patients in the past. It usually came from trouble in the home. Maybe she's missing Jay. He had been away a lot lately. I made a mental note to talk to him about his schedule when he got home.

Speaking of Jay, this would have been a great time for him to be home. We could have had a little fun. I got out car and grabbed my plate of food smiling to myself; I would finally be able to enjoy a meal in peace. As I headed to the door I noticed a large box sitting in front of the door. I checked it out and it was addressed to Mrs. Sasha Hayward-Duncan. I found it odd because I didn't use the name Hayward much. I picked it up and took it in the house. Once I was inside I sat the package down to set my alarm. I took my food in the kitchen and heated it in the microwave. As I waited my mind went back to the package in the hallway. Although I was starved, my curiosity was getting the best of me. I hurried down the hall to retrieve the package. I carried back to the kitchen and placed it on the counter to open it. Inside was a gift box from Build a Bear Workshop. There was also a card enclosed. I opened the card and it had a hand written message.

"Even though we are far apart...My love for you has grown greater and we'll be back together soon, sooner than you could imagine. Our love is eternal. Happy Mother's Day."

There was no signature. I smiled. I sat the box down and ran upstairs to my room. I was so eager that I didn't even look at the gift. I busted through the door expecting to see Jay, but he wasn't there. I checked throughout the whole house. No Jay. I was puzzled. He had to be somewhere around. There was no postal or UPS deliveries on Sundays. The alarm from the microwave disturbed my thoughts. I went back to the kitchen removed the food from the microwave and dumped it in the trash. My appetite was gone. I sat for a few moments staring at the box. It had to be more to it. I opened the build a bear box and it contained a bear with the words Honey Brown stitched on the t-shirt. My heart began to pound rapidly. I turned the bear around, to see if anything was attached.

Nothing.

I looked at the bear again.

"Honey Brown?" I said aloud.

That's what Lorenz used to call me. I threw the bear across the room. I ran to the phone and dialed Jay's number. It went straight to voice mail. I slammed the phone down and a lump formed in my throat. Everything seemed to be closing in around me and I began to lose my breath. I was experiencing a serious panic attack. I tried to mentally coach myself as I would with my patients.

Calm down Sasha. Breathe-Breathe…

It wasn't working. Tears streamed down my face as sharp pains pounded in my chest. I managed to make my way into the living room. I lay in a fetal position on my couch waiting for this agonizing moment to pass.

"Sasha-Saa-shaaa…"

I opened my eyes at the mention of my name. I sat up quickly and searched the room with my eyes. I was alone. Then I heard it again.

"Saashaa…" The voice grew louder and echoed throughout the house. It was a familiar voice a calming voice. It seemed to be coming from the direction of the basement. I crept over to the door and the voice spoke again.

"I'm down here. I've been waiting for you." It said.

I opened the door and headed down the steps. For some reason I was drawn to this voice like metal to a magnet. I reached the bottom and my eyes widened in surprise. It couldn't be. There was no way possible that it could be.

"Lorenz?" I asked in disbelief.

He grinned devilishly, "Of course…Who else did you expect it to be?"

Tears poured down my face. I had to be dreaming this wasn't real. Lorenz was dead.

"I'm dreaming-I have to be dreaming. You're not real! You're dead!" I screamed. "You're dead!"

He began to walk over to me and I attempted to back away. However my body was numb. I couldn't move. It was as if I was super glued to the surface.

We were now face to face. He was even more beautiful than I remembered. His dark body was chiseled in all the right places. He still smelled of Chrome the cologne he used to wear faithfully.

"Sasha if I were dead would I be able to do this?"

He grabbed a fistful of my hair from the back and kissed me roughly, thrusting his tongue in my mouth. I felt myself sinking deeply into his brutal passion. I began to kiss him back with force.

In my mind I knew this could not be really happening but my body was telling me otherwise. He ripped my clothes off like a savage beast and gazed at my body with hunger in his eyes.

I was more than willing to satisfy his hunger. The throbbing between my legs became intense and my eagerness made itself known as my sweet love nectar prematurely made an escape down my inner thighs.

Without haste he attacked me like a mad man. I lay on the floor as he devoured my forbidden fruit sucking, licking, slurping like it was the last meal he'd ever partake in.

Deep moans of satisfaction escaped my quivering lips as he spread my pussy apart. Three fingers were now probing me gently while my clit was being tickled by his thumb. My hips were now gyrating to his rhythm. My erect nipples were being catered to as he sucked away causing milk to flow. Reality escaped my mind as he took me far, far away to a magical place; where nothing mattered but him and I.

He gazed into my eyes as if he could see right through me.

"I love you Sasha, soon we will be a family again."
Then he began to fade away.
"Wait don't go! Please don't go. I love you Lorenz!"

Chapter 4

"What did you call me?" He snapped. I opened my eyes and Jay was standing over top of me in my living room.
I sat up quickly.
"Jay? What-when did you get here?" I was baffled.
I scanned the area and realized it was all a dream. I must have passed out from the attack.
He backed away from me. "You just called me Lorenz Sasha!"
"No...No why would I do that" I lied.
I was fantasizing about my dead abusive husband; which was not a good thing. To make it worse my current husband witnessed it, and I called him by his name. How was I going to get out of this? Think Sasha think. It was no use I dropped my head in defeat. There was no way I could make an excuse for my actions.
"I'm sorry Jay. Things have been crazy around here."
I rubbed the back of my neck. It was stiff. My whole body was sore. It was almost as if the encounter had truly happened. I was so ashamed that I could barely look him in the face.
"I can see that! I walk in my home to surprise my wife on Mother's Day. Instead of hugs and kisses I'm greeted by my wife masturbating and calling out another man's name! A man that raped and abused you! A man that you claim to *hate* so much!"

For the first time I noticed the flowers and Tiffany's bag on the coffee table. Tears began to cascade down my face. If he were here none of this would be happening. I was beginning to get angry. He had been gone almost a week. He had no clue what was going on.

"Baby I'm sorry. You don't understand what's been happening around here. I been having strange calls, strange gifts have been popping up. Azariah is not the same. We need you here! You haven't been here for us!" I cried out.

He plopped down in the chair in front of me and threw his hands in the air. He laughed slightly.

"You got to be fucking kidding me! You're blaming this on me? So it's my fault that you're having sex dreams about your low life baby dad! It's my fault that I'm trying to make a living to provide for my family!"

I knew it was a problem now. He was cursing, something he rarely did. I understood the point he was trying to make but he still was not hearing what I was saying.

"Jay you're missing the point. Something wrong is going on here. Azariah is being disrespectful. Bracelets, Teddy bears, pictures and strange notes are appearing. What you walked in on was nothing but the erratic behavior of how these events are affecting me. There is no question about it. I do hate the things that Lorenz did to me. But over the years I have come to realize that he was a sick man. His actions were not his fault. His circumstances pushed him into a deep depression and that was the way he lashed out. He needed help."

I couldn't believe that I just defended him out loud. This speech played out over and over in my mind for years. I was tired of everyone blaming him for everything. We all played a part in his demise, including me. I should have just been honest with him from the start and maybe things could have been different. Don't get me wrong, I loved Jay with all of my heart. But Lorenz and I did share something special. Something no one would ever understand, not even myself.

Jay just stared at me with a blank look on his face as if he couldn't find the words to speak. I know me taking up for Lorenz was tripping him out. But it had to be said. Enough was enough. I decided to continue on while I had a chance.

"Honestly Jay, I really don't understand why you have to work as many hours as you do. We aren't pressed for money. This house is paid-"

"No you need to rephrase that...*You* aren't pressed for money. This is *your* house that your ex-father-in-law and *lover* paid for. How do you think that makes me feel!"

"Every day I am reminded of the Haywards; this house, the businesses and Azariah. All belong to them. I wish with all my heart that I was her biological father."

I was stunned. I had no idea that he felt that way. Jay was jealous. He didn't give two shits of what was going on around here. He was too busy having a pity party that I would not have any part of.

"Jay you knew all of this before you married me. If you weren't secure with yourself, maybe you shouldn't have asked me to be your wife. Maybe you should have provided a place for us seven years ago, so you wouldn't have to live in my *lover's* home." I spat.

I stood up and went to the kitchen to get the note and bear. When I returned he was sitting in the same spot with a solemn look on his face. I dropped the note and bear in his lap.

"Get over yourself Jay and save your family before something happens."

Chapter 5

I lay in bed alone thinking about the heated discussion that occurred between Jay and I. Shortly after I left him sitting in the living room, I heard the front door slam and his truck peel off in a hurry. At the time I didn't feel bad about what I said. However six hours and many crying spells later, guilt was beginning to come into play. I had to put myself into his shoes. How would I feel if I came home and caught him masturbating and calling out his ex's name?

Pissed.

Hurt.

Betrayed.

That's how I would feel. I figure he was experiencing the same emotions. I thought about what he said about being constantly reminded of the Haywards. I guess he had a point there too. I was now used to living a lavish style of life. In the beginning Jay made decent money, but it was pennies compared to the empire Dr. Gregory Hayward had secretly built. An empire that now belonged to me. I know it seems selfish, but I was dealt a bad hand in life. It just so happen that God realized that he reneged and I was dealt a new hand, a winning hand. It would be foolish to throw it in now. I needed to find a way to make my wrongs right.

***

The next morning, I woke up to breakfast in bed. Jay leaned over and kissed me softly on the lips.

"Morning baby…."

His breath smelled of mint and liquor. He must have had a rough night because the toothpaste couldn't hide the stench of whiskey. I managed to smile. I felt a little uneasy. I just prayed that he didn't get pissy drunk and do something he may regret. More so I hope my adulterous performance didn't push him to seek some random pussy.

"I see you hung out with *Jack* last night. I hope you and *Mr. Daniels* behaved yourselves." I said in a joking manner.

I was serious as hell.

He chuckled a little, "We were on our best behavior."

I gave him a look as if he was lying.

He held up two fingers, "Scouts honor."

He had this ridiculous boyish look on his face. I couldn't help but laugh. I moved the tray of food to the night stand and kissed him on the lips.

"Baby I am so sorry for the things I said. I was just so worked up about everything that was going on. I love you, and only you. I don't know what came over me yesterday –"

"Sash, stop. That was yesterday. This is a new day. We need to leave the past in the past or we will not have a future. Baby I have no future without you. I love you unconditionally. You and our children are my life." He was sincere. He held my face in his hands gently.

My eyes were swollen and red from my all night cry session. The tears were beginning to form again causing my eyes to burn.

"I can't see myself without you either." My voice was beginning to crack. "I love you and appreciate you so much. You're an amazing person and sometimes I feel like I don't deserve you."

I removed his hands from my face and pulled his close to mine. I kissed his forehead, lips and drop light kisses on his chest. I felt him begin to grow as I helped him slide out of his boxers. I slid out of my nightie and buried my head under the blankets to show my *friend* how much I appreciated him. I slowly rolled my tongue up and down his shaft as I took of him in my mouth. I flicked my tongue around his opening. He began to take deep breathes moaning as he experienced pure pleasure. He gently pushed my head down further signaling me to take him all the way in. I aim to please. I was going all the way in. I wrapped my lips around his pole and suctioned him in like a Dirt Devil. I gave him a little dick to tonsil action. I had built up so much moisture in my mouth that it was seeping from the sides. It ran down my chin and hit his balls. I decided it was time for them to get some attention. I let him slide from my mouth and engulfed my mouth with his is balls. I cautiously hummed on them. His legs began to tremble and I felt his warm juices run down the side of my face.

He lifted me up and placed me across the bed. He split my legs apart into a wide V-shape. He lowered his head until I could feel his breath against my lips. He parted them with his tongue, and sucked each one until they were swollen. I closed my eyes, grabbed on the sheets and held my breath. He tickled my clit with his nose as he began to taste me. My *girl* began to throb. But not like it usually does. For some reason Lorenz popped back into my mind. I tried to shake it and focus on, Jay but it was no use. It was Lorenz I was seeing that caused me to become even wetter. Jay was about to explode again; the extra moistness was causing a smacking sound every time he dove deep into me. He thought I had climaxed but I didn't. The thought of being with Lorenz made me excited. I would never tell him the truth. That would bruise his ego. I tried to block him out of my mind and concentrate on Jay, but it wasn't working.

I moved his head from between me, and got on all fours and told him to do it from the back. He was a little shocked, because I didn't like doing it that way anymore. It reminded too much of Lorenz and Greg, that's the way they loved it. They were about being in control. Part of me loved to be dominated. Jay hadn't seen that side of me since the night we first met in Florida. Tonight I was going to re-introduce him to an old friend that I had imprisoned many years ago.

When he entered me, I closed my eyes and thought about Lorenz. I felt my pussy begin to throb like it used to back then; I began to throw my ass back on his dick. I think I almost knocked him off the bed. I was working my hips and throwing my ass at him so hard. Jay tried to keep it together and gain control. After a few strokes he came hard.

I acted as if I came too. I was a little disappointed. I guess he thought he really worked it out. He climbed up in the bed and within a few minutes he was snoring. I went to the bathroom to really get my thing off. I reminisced about the first time I ever had sex with Lorenz back in Greg's office. I pleasured myself until I felt the wet stickiness flow out. I tried to hold in the moans from my climax. I didn't want to wake Jay. I went to the sink to wash my hands but I couldn't even look at myself in the mirror. I had mentally cheated on my husband...again.

Chapter 6

"So...what made you have no idea who could have sent that bear? He asked as he took a bite of his cheesesteak.

We were sitting on the patio enjoying our take out dinner. Mom Duncan decided to keep the kids until the morning. She must have sensed that we needed time alone.

I sat my fork down. "I honestly have no idea. Lorenz was the only one who called me by that name and he had given me a similar gift when we first started dating. The only people who knew about the nickname are either dead or no longer a part of my life."

"I read the little note that was left with the package. It made me think. I mean really think. I read it over and over again. I came to the conclusion that it has to be someone in your past trying to mess with your mind. Or it's you trying to get my attention." He said nonchalantly.

Again he managed to say some off the wall shit to make my blood boil. You would have thought after the amazing morning and even more amazing afternoon he wouldn't say something so hurtful.

"Boy you are a piece of work." I had to laugh it off to calm myself.

I wanted to take my food and throw it in his face. How dare he accuse me of doing such a heinous act. Who in their right mind would fake a stalking?

"I mean really Sasha who would go through all of this trouble to stalk you or Azariah? What the hell would they get out of toying with a little girl? Not to mention spend a few thousand on an iced out charm bracelet. No one I know has money to blow like that but *you.* If you want my attention you got it. I'm all yours." He smiled.

"You know what, Fuck you Jay! What do you think I'm some type of nut job that I would go through all of this to get attention? I hate to break it to you baby you are not all that for me to do some looney shit. Humph, for all I know you just may be the one who's doing it. It's kind of funny that you show up the same day as the package and you just so happen to hear me say I love Lorenz. Did I really say that Jay? Or is that something you made up to make me admit my true feelings?" He had sparked a nerve and I was on the roll.

"Fuck me? Naw, I know you didn't say fuck me. You know what fuck you!" He knocked everything off the table and stormed into the house. I knew his feelings were hurt I never talked reckless to him. Again the guilty feeling came back. I needed to fix this. I ran in the house behind him. I caught him as he was about to head out the door.

"Jay wait! Don't go, please." I begged.
He turned to me biting his lip. His nose was flared and his eyes wear tearing.

"Tell me you swear to God that you didn't buy the bracelet, or get me that bear." I was looking into his eyes to see if I could see any deceit.

He reached for my hand, and gazed deeply into my eyes. "Sash, I didn't have anything to do with any of this. I can't lie to you and make you hear what you want. This madness has to stop. If you don't trust me or can't be truthful with me, we can't go on. I'm starting to not know who you are anymore. I don't know if it's post-partum depression that you are going through or what?"

I wrapped my arms around his waist. We walked back to the living room together and sat on the couch. I laid across his lap as he stroked my hair.

"Who's doing this to us?" I said quietly.

"I really don't know. Like I said it has to be someone from your past. Shit for all we know it could be Starla playing a sick joke. It's not like she comes from a stable family. Camille was a nut and you already know what my thoughts are about Gregory."

Starla? Was he out of his mind?

How could he think she would do something like this? That girl helped us out in a major way years ago. I immediately became defensive again. I was starting to think I was Bi-polar the way my moods were switching up.

"Jay! How could you think that Starla would do something so cruel? She has been a part of this family for years. If she wanted to do something to hurt us; I believe it would have been done years ago. You do realize that she lost her mother by helping us?"

I moved from his lap and scooted away from him. He was really turning me against him.

He rolled his eyes and stood up in front of me, "Exactly, she lost her mother. I think she's jealous of what we have. She always has been. Haven't you noticed how uneasy she acts around me? She only deals with you and Azariah. She treats Lil' Jay like he doesn't exist."

His whole demeanor changed. Hate was in his tone as he continued to bash an innocent young lady. He really had it in for all of them. I had to admit I was really confused. He never showed an inkling of dislike towards Starla when she would visit. I thought he truly cared about her. He treated her as one of the family.

"I'm sorry that you feel that way. You should have told me this years ago and we could have discussed it. But it's not Starla. There is no way she would do something like this. Besides she was a child when all of this was going on. I have my money on Shelly. She is the only one who would have something to gain from all of this."

I had spoken without thinking and didn't realize what had come out of my mouth.

. "Shelly?" he laughed. "Babe when is the last time you've seen her? She doesn't even know where you are besides what would she get out of it. It seems to me she has everything you have. You both have babies by that bastard. The only thing she didn't get was the money. Oh so that's it she wants her child to be heir of the Hayward fortune." He was being sarcastic.

I snickered at his ignorance. He was trying to be smart but the thing is he was partially wrong. Shelly and I had nothing of the same. Her child was truly a Hayward and entitled to everything that was left to my child. It had to be Shelly behind this there was no question about it. I was determined to prove it.

Chapter 7

Two days had gone by and I was still unable to get a hold of Starla. I tried her cell phone and called her home. I left several messages and none of my calls were returned. I was feeding Sarai when I heard the front door slam. It startled us and the baby began to cry.

"Where's Azariah?" he snapped. He was breathing hard, and sweating.

"Well good evening to you too. She's in her room...why?"

He ignored me and ran up the steps. I wanted to run after him to see what was going on, but I couldn't leave the babies alone with Lil' Jay. I sat there for a few seconds until I heard a bunch of yelling. Something wasn't right I needed to see what was up. I sat Sarai in her bouncer and strapped her in. I turned Cartoons on for them and ran up the steps. I could hear Azariah whimpering. I picked up my pace and busted in her room. Jay had his belt in his hand and Azariah was lying across the bed with whelps across her thighs. I was hot. He hit my damn child. I pushed Jay.

"Are you losing your damn mind? Why did you hit her?" I was livid. He looked as if he was about to smack the shit out of me.

"You know she disrespected my mother? Huh...did you know that she was over there showing her ass, talking to my mother, the woman who helped raise her, and looked out for her before she was even born like she was nothing! She was talking about stuff she had no idea knowing about. I know ain't nobody but that damn Starla put all that shit in her head."

He turned back to Azariah and continued to whack her across the bottom with his thick leather belt. I couldn't believe what was going on. I balled up my fist and began punching him in his head.

"Get the hell off of my child you bastard!" I yelled as I wailed on his head. He diverted his attention from her and grabbed me by the throat. He pinned me against the wall and began choking me.

"You gonna come up here trying to defend her. She deserved every bit of that ass whooping. If she does it again, it will be worse, and if you ever put your hand on me again...."

I could fill the spit flying on my face. He was foaming at the mouth like a mad man. He stood there with his teeth clenched. My heart was beating a mile a minute. Memories of the abuse I suffered from Lorenz resurfaced. I closed my eyes and silently prayed that he wouldn't hit me. God must have heard me, because when I opened them he was gone.

I ran over to Azariah and wrapped my arms around her and we both cried together. The kids and I all slept together in Azariah's room that night. Jay never returned home. He had Chuck come by and gather his things he needed for his business trip. He left me a voicemail apologizing for his actions. He said he was definitely out of character and he would make it up to us. He promised to take us on a family vacation the day after Memorial Day. That made me feel a little better. We could use the vacation. I told Azariah about the trip and she didn't respond.

Over the days she had become distant. Not talking to anyone. She didn't even interact with her siblings. She went to school came home and went straight to her room. The only time she would come out would be to eat and then she would only pick at her food. I had to face the hard facts that my child was officially depressed. My heart pained at the site of her. Her glow was diminishing. I needed to get her help before things got worse. I thought about letting one of my colleagues

34

talk with her but my pride wouldn't allow it. I decided to call my dad to see if he could talk to Azariah.

I checked the time it was now after three so that meant he was most likely still at one of his clothing stores. I wasn't sure if he was in Charlotte or Fayetteville I decided to call his cell phone. The phone rang several times just when I was about to hang up, he answered the phone.

"What's up baby girl?" he sounded a little winded.

"Hey Daddy are you ok?" I was concerned by the way he sounded. Lately he had been having issues with his breathing. His weight and the fact that he smoked a pack of Newports a day, oh yeah, and let's not forget his daily "herbal medication" that he partakes in several times a day, were all a factor in his condition. I tried several times to get him to get healthy and kick his habits but it fell upon death ears. It didn't help that no one else in the family seemed to care enough to help me get him on the right path. With no support I was fighting a no win situation so I backed off.

"I'm good Babe just a little tired that's all. So what's up? How's my babies?"

"That's what I'm calling you about. Azariah is going through something. She's not herself and matter of fact we are all going through something...."

I explained to him everything that went on starting the day of Azariah's party. I told him everything except the part about me fantasizing about my ex-husband. He listened to everything I had to say. He was pissed about Jay putting his hands on us. He said that he loved Jay like a son but would not tolerate the hitting bullshit. He made it clear that if it happened again that Jay could very well meet the same fate of Lorenz.

Unlike Jay my father took the stalking serious and said he would have a few of his "boys" look into the situation. I then thought maybe it wasn't the best idea to involve my father in my home life. He was over protective with all of his girls. But for some reason he was extra protective of me. I guess it was because he missed out on so many years. This weekend he was going to pickup Azariah and spend the day with her.

Hopefully he would be able to break through the shell she had put up and find out what's really going on.

When I hung up from my father I noticed my BlackBerry vibrating on my night stand. I had an email from Jay. I checked it. It was a message informing me that he wouldn't be back until the weekend of the trip. That was two weeks away. I couldn't help but to wonder if he was purposely staying away from us because of the Azariah incident. I picked up the phone to call him and as usual it went straight to voicemail. I began to feel nauseas.

Dear God please watch over my husband. Keep his mind and please don't let him do anything that would cause our family to break up.

That was my prayer. I don't know what I would do without my husband. I loved him so much and couldn't see my life going forward without him.

***

The next two days dragged. I received a brief call from Jay nightly. The conversations were short and impersonal. More like check in calls than anything. Sometimes I had to repeat myself twice just to get an 'I Love you' back.

It was Saturday and my dad had just left with Azariah. Today she seemed a little more upbeat. She even looked cute. She wore a banana terry cloth halter dress with a bronzy pair of gladiator sandals. Her hair was pulled back into a neat ponytail. I had to give it to her, to be only seven she was on point with keeping her appearance up. I went over to hug her but she just gave me a quick wave and hurried out the door. I tried not to feel some type of way about it. I was just happy that she was feeling better.

I was out back with the children when I heard someone call my name. I wasn't expecting anyone. I turned towards my patio door and my Aunt Rosa was coming through.

"Auntie Rosa!" Lil' Jay screamed as he ran towards her. He was excited to see her. I was glad too but I didn't expect her to be here until next week. She was going to watch the

36

babies while I went back to work. The older kids were going to camp at the church.

"Hey Aunt Rosa...I wasn't expecting you to be here this soon." I hugged her.

She kissed my cheek.

"Well I didn't expect to be here this soon. I had a talk with Mixxon and he asked me to come earlier. He didn't tell you?" She asked with a raised eyebrow.

I sighed and smiled. I should have known my dad had something to do with this.

"No but it doesn't matter you're here now and honestly I could use the company."

I sat down at the table and poured a glass of tea. I offered Aunt Rosa a glass she declined. She had a seriousness in her eyes; the same look that my dad gives when he is about to turn it out.

"So where is Jay?"

I couldn't look in her the eyes. I didn't even want to answer the question. But I know that wasn't going to be an option.

"He's working."

"Working?" she asked in nonbelief. "Working where and for how long?"

"He's on a business trip. He'll be back in about a week in a half. He's really been trying to make sure that we are financially stable. He feels bad for being away. He planned a weekend getaway for us when he comes back. That way we can have family time before I go back to work." I tried to make everything sound innocent.

She wasn't buying it. "Look I usually don't get into people's personal affairs. However my brother, your father told me what you told him. Sasha baby I know you love Jay, I love him too. But I will not tolerate him or anyone else harming my family. I don't care what Azariah did he had no business beating her like that. Nor did he have any business putting his hands on you!" she was heated.

I hurried to his defense, "Auntie it wasn't that bad. He gave her a regular spanking. I was just shocked to see him do it because he never hit her before and I hit him first. He was just trying to get me off of him. Really he wasn't trying to hurt us. He didn't even hit me. He just grabbed me up a little bit. It was nothing serious. Honest." I plead my case.

She just shook her head in disappointment.

"Be careful baby. You know what happened with Azariah's father. I would just hate to see that happen to you again. This time you may not be so lucky." She stood up.

"I'm going to put my bags away and take a nap. I'll speak with you later." She walked away without looking back.

The words *This time you may not be so lucky* played in my head over and over like a broken record. I just hoped she was wrong. But something deep inside lead me to believe otherwise.

Chapter 8

Two weeks had flown by quickly. Aunt Rosa spent most of the time with the children which left me with free time of my own. Jay was due back home later in the evening. Then tomorrow we would leave to go on our mini-vacation. I decided to take a trip to Durham to do a little shopping at the North Gate Mall. I myself preferred Crab Tree but Xiomara complained about the drive and since she lived not even five minutes away from the mall, North Gate was it.

I pulled into the parking lot and drove around until I found a decent spot. I had on a ridiculous pair of heels and refused to walk longer than I had to in them. Don't get me wrong, I could handle the heel long enough to get where I was going and take a seat. But walking around for hours on end or dancing the night away in them was not happening. I believe the shoe is a form of decoration something to sit and look pretty in. Today that's exactly what I planned to do, to sit and be cute. I turned my car off and pulled out my cell phone to let her know I had arrived. I dialed her number and waited for her to answer. I was drumming my fingers across the steering wheel when I noticed her.

"It can't be!" I said out loud.

I removed my sunglasses to get a clearer look.

My jaw dropped in astonishment. It was her. But how?

I opened the car door and ran towards the woman. She had already made her way into the mall. I was about to follow her until I heard my name being called.

"Sasha! Hey Sash aren't you forgetting something?"

I looked back and Xiomara was standing next to my car with my keys in purse in her hand.

Damn.

I turned my attention back towards the door and she was gone.

I ran over to Xiomara grabbed my purse slung it over my shoulder. I took a hold of her hand and dragged her to the entrance of Macy's. I was hoping I would be able to catch up with her.

Xiomara backed up to complain, "Damn Sash slow the hell down shit!"

I wasn't hearing anything she was saying. I pulled her through the department store searching like a mad woman. She finally had enough and broke away.

"Stop!" she yelled causing people to now stare at us.

"What the hell is wrong with your crazy ass?"

I didn't have time to explain I just wanted her to come on.

"Mara please just come on. I'm going to lose her! She's going to get away?" I was in panic mode.

She placed her hand on her hip and stared at me in confusion.

"What…who is getting away?"

It was a no win situation. I had to come clean if I wanted her to budge. I sighed and took a deep breath. I know she wouldn't believe me but I said it anyway.

"Camille! Mara, Camille is here in North Carolina. In this mall right now, I saw her. I swear to God I saw her!" I was hysterical.

She looked me over as if I was crazy and waved me off. She walked over to the Carol's Daughter counter and began to browse through the products. I followed her over.

"I know it sounds crazy but it was her. I know it was. It looked just like her she just seemed to be a bit younger. But it was Camille. I will never forget her face."

She continued to looking. "I would believe you. However Camille is doing a ten year sentence for manslaughter in Delaware. Oh and did you forget that Lover Boy Lorenz fucked up that pretty face of hers before he left her for dead." She handed the saleswoman her items and waited for them to be rung up.

I thought about it for a moment. She did have a point. I forgot all about her accident. So that couldn't have been Camille. I laughed to myself. I knew I had to look like a complete idiot running through the parking lot and the mall like a lunatic. I decided to drop the subject and do what I came to do shop!

A few hours and many shopping bags later, I was ready to go. I enjoyed the time spent with my sister. It seemed as if all of my problems were out the door. It was always like that with Xiomara she was a firecracker but had a good heart and was fun to be with. We were laughing and talking as she walked me to the car. I sat my bags on the hood of the car and looked through me purse for the keys. After a quick sweep I didn't find them. I didn't get upset because I didn't check thoroughly. I walked to the back of the car and emptied the contents of my purse on top of the trunk. Still no keys.

"What's wrong?"Xiomara asked.

"I –I can't seem to find my keys."

"Well what did you do with them? I handed them to you when I gave you the purse." She said.

I thought about it. I remembered her giving me the purse but I don't ever remember her handing me the keys.

"No-No ma'am you didn't give me the keys. I remember you giving me the purse then I grabbed your hand. I never got the keys. You still have them." I said in a matter of fact manner.

She rolled her eyes and searched her purse.

41

"Ummm, actually I did give them to you because they are not here. I don't have your keys."

I was now pissed. This hussy lost my keys and she was trying to pin the blame on me. I looked through the window of my car.

Nothing.

"Damn Mara you done lost my fucking keys and I have to pick my husband up from the fucking airport in less than an hour." I was beyond angry. Who told you to grab *my* things out of *my* car anyway?"

She wrinkled her face up, "Hold up bitch I know you're upset about your keys. But don't talk that crazy shit to me. You were the one running chasing after ghost from your past like a damn psycho path. I'm not the one who gets caught masturbating and calling out other niggas name while my husband is fucking me!"

Did she say what I just think she said?

"Excuse me?"

"You heard what the fuck I said. You got a lot of shit with you Ms. Lady. You play that innocent role but you are on some other shit. You can save that innocent for someone who don't know better. I don't blame Jay for staying away the way he does. Keep it up and you're gonna lose his ass for good." She stooped down and grabbed something that was next to the back tire.

"Here's your keys. Next time look carefully before you accuse someone of something." She turned sharply and walked away leaving me standing there alone.

I was hurt and embarrassed. I couldn't believe that Jay had shared that information with Chuck. That was personal.

I popped the trunk and threw the bags inside. I shut it and unlocked my car doors. I had a strange feeling that someone was watching me. I looked around and didn't see in anyone. I shook it off and pulled off.

Chapter 9

"Everybody got what they need" Jay asked as he shut the trunk to the Denali. The kids shouted, "yes!"

I was kissing my babies goodbye.

Aunt Rosa shooed me away. "These babies are in good hands, she said. We will be fine...You just go have fun."

"Ok, I will call you to check on them hourly" I said walking to the truck.

Jay shook his head at Aunt Rosa. "I'll take the cell from her if she gets out of control" he laughed. He got in the truck; I made sure all the kids had their seat belts on. I waved bye to Aunt Rosa as we drove off.

Last night when I picked Jay up from the airport he was in a great mood. Something I hadn't seen in a while so I decided not to bring up the argument I had with Xiomara.

I was also shocked at the way Aunt Rosa treated him. I was sure that she would have had a few words. Azariah even welcomed him with opened arms. I was happy that some sense or normality was coming back into my family. Halfway down the road I asked the kids what movie they wanted to watch while we were driving.

The both yelled "The Wiz!"

I sighed and put the movie in. Jay laughed. He just didn't understand. I have been breathing and dreaming "The Wiz" for the last few weeks. The church's youth department was putting on a play at the church. Zar had been chosen to play

43

Glenda the good witch. I was just happy to see that she was already coming back to herself.

I picked up my cell to call Sephira to let her know we were on our way. She was Jay's seventeen year old cousin. She and another girl from the church named Kim were tagging along with us to look after the children. As soon as the girls got in the car, they were hyped to see The Wiz was on. Kim had landed the role as Dorothy, so you know she sang every time Diana Ross did. Thank God for ear plugs.

***

A little over four hours later we arrived to our destination. We stayed at the Sea Watch Resort. I loved this place; it had everything. Jay had made all of the reservations, so I figured he got the 3 bedroom suite we always got. To my surprise, he had given the kids there own room. We were staying in a room across the hall. I was cool with that. Everyone grabbed their bags and headed to the rooms. Jay went to get his golf clubs and a few other things he had left in the car. I went to the kid's room to lay down a few ground rules. I told them no room service. No boys and my children had to be in bed by 9:30p.m., so they needed to at least be back in the hotel room by 9:00 o'clock. I told them we would go to dinner every evening around 5:00p.m. These were good girls so I knew I didn't have much to worry about. Kim asked if they could unpack later because they wanted to hit the water slides. I told them to go ahead.

I headed back to my room. I opened the door and Jay was talking low on his cell phone. I slowly walked in trying not to make any noise.

I heard him say, "This is not a good time...Yes...I understand... I'm doing everything you want me to do!" he slammed his phone shut. He turned around and jumped. He didn't realize I was there. "Hey baby...you scared me...I didn't know you were in here," he kissed me softly on my lips and ran his hand under my shirt cupping my breast. "I love you so much," he moaned.

I pushed his hand away. He wasn't getting off that easy.

"Jay, who was that on the phone?" I demanded

He tried to play it off as if it were nothing, "Oh that was one of my partners. Chris you remember him right? Well he wanted me to cut my vacation short. He needed me to go close a deal in New York Thursday but I told him that I was spending time with my family," he said then slipped his tongue in my mouth before I could say anything else. He began to kiss and caress me in all the right places.

Before I knew it he had me sprawled across the bed with his head between my thighs. I loved it and he knew it.

Later that evening we all met downstairs in the restaurant for dinner. The children talked non-stop about the water slides. They had their entire day planned out. They talked so much they barely touched there food.

I called to check on the babies. Everything was fine. Jay told me he wanted to hit the golf course early the next morning. I told him to knock himself out. I was going to sleep in. That night we went at it like a couple of teenagers. He tried to get me on the balcony so he could hit it doggie style, but memories of Greg flooded my mind.

"No babe I love the way you do me. We don't need to add all that extra stuff." I assured him.

"What do you mean? We are on vacation. We're supposed to be having fun. Come on Sash no one is going to see us. We are way on the twenty-first floor." He begged.

I hated to make my husband beg for his pussy. It was *late* night and we were way up here. I figured it would be fun and I could make a new memory with the man I love so that other one could go straight to the pit of hell where it belonged. I undressed and slid out the patio doors. The wind blew gently causing my nipples to become erect. I felt his arms wrap around my waist and his tool was pressed between the crack of my ass. I reached back and felt him. He was attempting to grow but needed a little help. I turned to face him and began to stroke him. Jay closed his eyes and groaned. There was a lounge chair on the deck. I thought about sitting in it to give him a little lip service. Instead I carefully got on my knees and took him deep inside my mouth. He grunted in pleasure as I locked my fingers around his tool and guided it back in forth in my mouth. He ran his fingers through my hair and stroked the side of my face as I orally made love to my "king". I felt myself getting wet. I loved pleasing my man. It was an extreme turn on that I could send him to a place of ecstasy with just a few flicks of the tongue.

Within a matter of minutes he had grown to his full length. He helped me to my feet and bent me over the railing. He spread my ass cheeks and slid his wet warm dick down the middle until it met the opening of my love cave. He plunged deep inside and stroked me nice and slow. It felt so good to have all of him inside me I closed my eyes and enjoyed the sounds of the crashing waves below along with the smacking sounds of my moistness. Jay was really showing off as he grinded deep inside me hitting my spot every so often causing me to go in a frenzy. He began to get excited and picked up his pace, smacking my ass. Jay was really putting work in. I began to get into the rhythm of things. He pushed himself deeper as I began to moan. Just when things were getting good he pulled out. He lifted me up and planted my body against the glass door. He dove deep inside and slow grinded me. I bit his neck in pure ecstasy; He began to move faster, bucking me against him. I started moaning his name. I closed my eyes and opened them back up. He was staring at me intensely, at my first glance. I saw Greg's face. I had to shake it off.

"I love you Sasha."

"I love you too…Jay."

With that being said we both let loose. We lay in the bed that night like two teenagers in love. I had finally gotten my old Jay back. I couldn't be happier. If that was true why was it that Lorenz and Greg were on my mind so strong.

Chapter 10

It was our last day at the resort. When I woke up Jay was nowhere to be found. I picked my cell phone up from the nightstand to check the time. It was a little after eleven o'clock. I must have really been tired. I climbed out of bed and went to the bathroom to freshen up. I turned on the faucet, retrieved my toothbrush from off the counter and began to squeeze the tooth paste when I heard the hotel phone ring. I began brushing my teeth as I went to answer it. I figured it was probably the children.

"Hey guys sorry I missed breakfast I over slept." I said with the toothbrush still in my mouth.

No response.

"Hello-can you hear me?" I removed the brush from my mouth.

I listened closer. It sounded as if I was hearing my echo. I spoke again to be sure.

"Hello...."

There was an echo and I could hear the water running through the phone. I threw the phone down and backed away. Someone was in the room.

"Oh shit...oh shit." I whispered. I didn't know what to do. The doors that led into the living room area were shut. That meant the other person had to be on the other side. I picked up my cell phone and called Jay. I heard a vibrating sound and noticed he had left his phone on the dresser. I was now scared.

I was stuck in the room with nowhere to run to. I thought about going to the balcony and screaming for help. But I was too far up for anyone to hear me. I crept in the bathroom keeping my eye on the door. Once inside I locked myself in and sat on the toilet watching the door. I decided to call the front desk to tell them someone was in my room. I dialed the number and realized that I didn't have a signal.

I tried hard not to cry but I couldn't help myself. I was scared and alone. No one was there to protect me. Just as I was about to lose it I heard footsteps coming to the door. I grabbed my metal nail file from off the counter and climbed into the tub. I closed the glass door and crouched down inside of it. I heard the door jingle followed by a loud knock. My body became stiff, it felt like something was fluttering in my stomach. Another loud knock came then I heard.

"Sasha? What are you doing? Open the door!"

It was Jay. I was relieved. I hurried to the door and opened it. I wrapped my arms around him and cried.
He hugged me back.

"Baby what's wrong? He said in a concerned voice as he rubbed my back.

"Someone was in here. I received a phone call there was no one there then I noticed that the phone echoed so I tried to see hang up and I couldn't someone was in the living room on the other phone. I tried to call for help and my cell was dead."

I spoke so fast that all my words ran together. Jay stared up me blankly like I was losing my mind. That's when he noticed the file in my hand.

He walked away from me rubbing his head as he sat on the edge of the bed. He sat there in deep thought for a few moments before he spoke.

"Babe I think you need to talk to someone when you go back to work." I was about to flip but he held his hand up motioning me to stop.

"Just hear me out. Something is not right. I don't know what it is with you. But ever since Zar's birthday you've been on some conspiracy theory shit. I tried to overlook it, I thought

48

this vacation would help but I was wrong. I received a call from Chuck yesterday he told me about the "Camille" sighting you supposable had. You are going too far with all of this. I don't know why this is happening or what you're trying to accomplish. I'm fed up and I want this to stop now! " He was clearly upset and meant business.

Again I felt betrayed.

Why was everyone treating me like I was some delusional nut case? I couldn't even look him in the face. I walked over to the other side of the bed and climbed in. I pulled the covers over my head and lay in silence. Shortly after, I heard the door slam. He was gone leaving me alone with my thoughts. I began to wonder if I really was going insane.

***

Later that afternoon I found myself sitting at the bar getting wasted. We were due to leave in a few hours. I refused to sit in my room and sulk. I was the victim and I was tired of everyone treating me like the culprit. The bartender handed me another glass of Ciroc Coconut and lemon-aid. Jay's words kept playing in my head. I couldn't believe he talked to me like that. I continued to sip on my drink. Before I knew it I had downed three more. I was really feeling it. I watched the other guest around me. They were all laughing, dancing and having a good time. I ordered one more drink and asked the bartender what my bill was. He told me that I was already paid up. I was baffled. I didn't remember paying. So I had to make sure he wasn't mistaken. I

"Hey are you sure about that? I'm a little torn up, but I think I would remember paying you."

He pointed to the other end of the bar and explained to me that there was a gentlemen who had been watching me that paid for it. His facial expression changed suddenly.

"What's wrong?" I inquired.

"The guy was just there like two minutes ago...."

"Don't worry about it I have an idea who it is anyway." I said with a sly smile. I gave him a nice tip and attempted to get up off the stool. Once I stood I realized how drunk I was because I almost lost my balance.

I took the elevator to my room, and I could barely stand up. I opened the door and practically fell in. I laughed at myself. I hadn't felt this way in years. I went into the bedroom, and Jay was in the bed snoring. I thought he was faking. He was just at the bar. Well...I guess he wasn't the one who bought the drinks. Oh well...I thought. Skipping out of my sundress and panties, I climbed on top of Jay. To my satisfaction he was naked. I kissed on his chest and headed to down yonder. My "friend" was asleep. I slipped him into my wet juicy mouth and he woke up quickly. Within minutes he had arose from the dead. I flicked my tongue along the vein leading to his thick mushroom shaped head. I sucked his juices that escaped early in my mouth. I deep throated him and put my neck in it.

I could see his toes curl up. He was pulling my hair and apologizing at the same time. I told him to turn over on his stomach and gave his ass some attention...he was in bliss. He was pulling sheets and everything. When I was finished he tried to return the favor. I told him I didn't want that. I told him I wanted him to fuck my ass. He was excited. That would be the first time that I ever let him do it that way. He tried to be real gentle with it. I yelled out for him to just fuck me like I was some bitch on the street. He was a little hesitant at first...I think my aggressiveness scared him. It didn't take him long to get with it and wear my ass out literally.

We both apologized and packed our bags.

Chapter 11

I was finally back to work. I had to admit I was glad to be back around adults and out of the house. I went to my office to see if I had any appointments scheduled. I had a 10 a.m. and nothing else until 3p.m. I was happy, that would give me time to catch up on paper work.

Around 1:30 my secretary Gazelle came to the door.

"Dr. Duncan...I'm sorry to bother you but there's a Ms. Conner here to see you. She said she was family," she whispered.

I froze immediately the only Conners I knew were Starla and Camille and I prayed that it was Starla. It seemed as if time had stood still. Gazelle cleared her voice to get my attention.

"Dr. Duncan are you alright?"

"Yes...I'm fine umm-send Ms. Conner in please." I had a sudden hot flash. I took a sip from the bottle of spring water that was sitting on my desk.

Gazelle gave me a look of uncertainty before she left out of the office. A few moments later my worst fear was standing in front of me.

"Camille?" I said.

"...And you know it." She strutted over to my desk and pulled a chair up making herself comfortable.

I couldn't believe my eyes. She looked great. I was confused.

"Camille…how-how can this be. I thought you, well you know I didn't expect you to look like this. How is it even possible that you are here? I-I thought you were sentenced to twelve years?"

She chuckled lightly, "Miss Sasha I see you are still naïve. Sweetheart there's nothing that money can't buy whether it's looks or freedom. As you should know, my late husband had plenty of it. That you and your makeshift family are enjoying right now." She crossed legs while she sneered at me.

I shifted in my seat. I was now uncomfortable when she mentioned Greg's money.

"What's wrong Miss Sasha? Did I strike a nerve?" She smiled wickedly.

"Camille why are you here? I have moved on with my life. I really don't want to go backwards. So much is going on right now and-"Then it came to me. Camille was behind everything that had been going on. I jumped out my seat.

"It's you! Oh my God! You have been the one stalking my daughter. You've been sending the gifts." I grabbed my phone to call Jay so he could know that I wasn't crazy. Camille was here and she was behind all of the madness that had been slowly tearing our family apart.

She then stood up and snatched the phone from me.

"If you know what's good for you. You will calm your silly ass down. Remember I know that little secret you've been hiding for the last seven years." She said sternly.

I quickly regained my composure and sat back down.

"Now you sit there and keep your fat mouth shut until I am done talking," she demanded. "As you know the life you are living is a fucking lie. You're stealing from a little boy who is rightfully entitled to everything your bastard child owns, including this plush office and shelter you have going on. Now I'm not going to lie. I hate Shelly for everything she's done. Thanks to her I had to go through four reconstructive surgeries on my face. Surgeries that depleted my life savings. Not to mention I had to pay for a ridiculously priced lawyer to get me off of those charges."

"Huh, get off? Jay told me you were sentenced to twelve years mandatory. He was there. He stayed during the whole trial." She must have thought I was stupid. I know she did time. Jay was there to make sure of it.

She began to laugh out loud, "Really Sasha…I feel sorry for you. Sweetness, your husband lied to you. He was definitely there. But he wasn't there for the reasons you believed. James Duncan was one of my lawyers. Your husband and his team made sure I didn't do a stitch of time honey. In fact I stayed six months at the Rockford center, paid a hefty fine and I was done."

This bitch was lying. Jay wouldn't do that I was so mad that I could spit; instead, I hauled off and slapped her as hard as I could.

"You lying Bitch! Get the Fuck outta here! My husband would never defend you! He fuckin hates you!" I was livid and yelling like a mad man.

My door flew open and Gazelle appeared. "Dr. Duncan do you need me to call someone?" She asked with her eyes glued on Camille.

"No Miss Lady she's fine. Now you need to go and do what you do sweetie before you have no job!" Camille barked.

"Gazelle I'm fine. Just do me a favor and cancel all of my afternoon appointments. After you're done you can go home early. I'm fine. There's just a few things I need to take care of."

She had an uneasy look on her face but she did as she was told. When she shut the door I got on Camille.

"You have no right talking to my Secretary that way."

"Fuck her! You need to listen and listen clearly. I have been beaten and left for dead, I lost my husband and my daughter thanks to you. You are a conniving bitch who seems to have everyone fooled everyone except me. The apple doesn't fall too far from the tree does it? You're no different than your whore mother. Karma came for her ass in the form

53

of cancer and she's coming for you on the form of Camille Conners!"

"Don't talk about my mother Camille! You can't blame this on me. You brought everything on yourself!"

"Sasha, I didn't deserve this. There was a time that I truly loved Greg. Your mother ruined him by coming back. We were fine before she came begging for his help to raise you. You took everything from me and now I'm taking everything from you!" she spat.

Tears were forming in her eyes part of me wanted to feel sorry for her. However my selfishness wouldn't allow it. She was threatening me. There was no way she was going to make me lose everything.

"How much do you want? A million…name your price." I logged onto my computer in case she wanted me to transfer money.

She rolled her eyes and shook her head.

"Do you think that you could throw me a few ends and I would disappear? Oh Miss Sasha nothing is ever that easy especially with me. I already know that a million dollars is really nothing to you. I've done my research honey. I don't even know why you or that husband of yours are even working. You could be traveling the world. I know that's what I attend to do with my portion."

"How much do you want?" I was tired of going back and forth with her. I just wanted her to go back under the rock she came from.

"What I want doesn't have a number attached to it. I want revenge and you're going to help me get it. I know you remember Shelly. Shelly, my once best friend and the best fuck I ever had, betrayed me. Well she fucked me royally by driving Lorenz to want to kill me. Now she's this happy homemaker married to a man who happens to own several mega churches. She has a few new brats and of course little Lorenz. Who just happens to be the true heir to your riches."

"Ok so she moved on with her life. Camille we all have so why is it so hard for you to do the same. I'm trying to make my wrongs right with you but you won't accept it."

"I'm not a charity case Sasha. I want that bitch to pay with her fucking life. She tried to take mine and I'm going to make sure she loses her!" she was full of hate and meant everything she said.

I couldn't believe what I was hearing. There was no way I was going to help her commit murder.

"Oh I'm sorry but I can't help you. There is no way I am going to help you kill Shelly. She's not one of my favorite people either but I wish death upon no one. I'm sorry your just gonna have to do what you have to do."

"Are you sure about that? Are you ready to lose everything? Your family, your lifestyle, or even your freedom? You know you falsified information? If I'm not mistaken that's a felony. So you could most likely end up in jail. I really don't think James would appreciate you hiding the fact that he was indeed that little girl's father. All in the name of money. Isn't his parents heavy in the church? Greed is one of the seven deadly sins right? I don't think they would be all that forgiving. I'm gonna give you a few days to think about this."

She stood up and went to the door. Before she walked out she said. "By the way this visit is between you and I. If you run your mouth all bets are off. Choose wisely Miss Sasha or lose everything."

Chapter 12

It had been two days since Camille's visit. I had been a nervous wreck. I cancelled all of my appointments for the week. I knew a few of my patients would probably go elsewhere. I didn't care. I was going through my own crisis. I replayed our conversation over and over in my head. I couldn't believe that she really thought I would help her kill Shelly. Another thing that messed me up was her saying that Jay was acting as her lawyer. I just couldn't believe that was true. Why would he do something like that? It just didn't make any sense.

That night when Jay called home to check in I wanted to confront him about it badly. I chose not to. I thought about Camille's threat but I did ask him would he ever keep anything from me. He seemed to catch a little attitude behind that question. I guess I would too if my husband questioned my trust. I apologized and let it go. I would find out the truth in due time.

There was a knock at my door. Before I could ask who it was Azariah came in. She had her cell phone in her hand.

"Mom can I go over Aunt Mara's she's taking her kids to Carolina Winds. She said that I can go if you let me."

"Zar you know that you have school tomorrow. Why is she going in the middle of the week anyway?" I was groggy from taking the Xanax pills I took from my job to calm my nerves.

She huffed and rolled her eyes, "How about the last day of school was two days ago. It's not the middle of the week, it's Thursday." She said with an attitude.

I sat up in my bed. I didn't remember going to the end of the year picnic. I go every year.

"What they didn't have the picnic this year?"

She was now irritated,. "Yes they did have it mommy. You couldn't go because you took to many of your little blue pills and wouldn't wake up. Aunt Rosa went instead."

"Oh shit! I'm so sorry Zar! Mommy hasn't been feeling to well and the pills help me feel better. Oh baby. I feel so bad."

I did feel bad. I had been popping those pills around the clock trying to get my mind right. I lost track of time. Damn. I wonder if Camille tried to get in touch with me. Fear began to set in. I prayed that she wouldn't stick to her word and ruin me.

"Can I go or not?" she asked again.

She was very rude, but I didn't care I had other things on my mind that were far more important than her little tantrum.

"Go ahead. I'll pack you an overnight bag in a few." I got out of the bed and went to my purse to get my cellphone.

"That's ok it's already packed. I will be back Sunday night…or never." She slammed the door behind her. I rolled my eyes. She was such a drama queen and I was not in the mood for it. I called my answering service to see if I had any messages. I had a few from my patients that I skipped, none from Camille.

I wondered what was up with her. I thought I would have heard from her by now. I went to the bathroom to freshen up. I noticed Jay's electric shaver on the counter. Was he home? I removed my robe from the back of the door and went down stairs. Aunt Rosa was making peanut butter and jelly sandwiches.

"Morning Aunt Rosa…."

She looked me up in down in disgust then went back to what she was doing.

I ignored her look and went over to the table and gave Lil' Jay a kiss on the forehead. He even had a funny look on his face. What the hell was going on? I looked around and realized my twins were not there.

"Aunt Rosa where are the babies?"
She walked over to the table and sat the plate of food in front of my son.

"They are with their father over at his mother's house." Her attitude was stank.

"Jay's home?"

She looked at me as if I were crazy, "Yes Sasha he came home late last night. He was ticked off because he had to catch a cab home from the airport."

"Why didn't he just call home? I would have picked him up." I began to fix myself a cup of coffee.

She snatched me by the arm causing the cup to fall to the floor. Lil' Jay began to cry when he heard the cup break.

"Aunt Rosa what the hell is wrong with you?" She pulled me down the hall into the living room. To be as small as she was she was quite strong.

"What's wrong with me is *you!* You've been absent as a mother for the last four days. When you came home from work Monday you were high as a kite and have been that way since. I don't know what is going on with you but it's affecting your children. Azariah's mouth is way out of control I caught her telling one of her friends on the phone that her mother pops blue pills and was too high to come to the picnic. I took her phone away and slapped her mouth for saying those things about you. Little Jay wants to know why his mommy is sleep all the time. The babies cry all the time. Last night I tried to talk to Jay about everything. He brushed me off. He was in his own little world. So he gets up this morning packs up the twins and Lil' Jay's things and said his mother will take care of his children since it bothered me so much. If you and your husband didn't want to be parents maybe you should have thought twice about having them."

"Why is Lil' Jay and Azariah still here?"

"Lil Jay cried to stay with me. I guess you didn't hear me clearly when I said he said he would take *his* children to his mothers. Azariah heard what he said and she called Xiomara and told her everything. It's not right for him to say things like that. When he married you he married her too she's part of you. He better watch himself before I let Mixxon know what's going on. It won't be nice for either of you. My brother loves his family. He'll die if he knew his daughter was turning into a druggie."

Druggie? Now she had gone overboard. I realize now that I may have been out of it for a few days. But I was not a damn addict. She was over stepping her boundaries.

"Look I understand that you're upset. What you're not gonna do is sit up in my fucking house and disrespect me or my husband for that matter. I appreciate you looking out for the kids while I've been under the weather. As far as Jay and I being parents, we were doing great before you came here and we'll be fine once you leave." I raised my eyebrow hoping she could read between the lines.

Her lips began to quiver, "Are you putting me out Sasha?" her voice began to crack. She was clearly upset.

"Not today. You need to know that whatever goes on in my house is none of my father's or anyone else's business. If you disrespect me or speak ill of my husband again you will leave me no choice but to ask you to leave."

Chapter 13

It was getting late and Jay still hadn't come back home from his mother's. Lil' Jay was asleep next to me in the bed. After my argument with Aunt Rosa I made him come to my room with me. He protested at first but after a few whacks on the back side he gave in and had been confined to my room ever since. I knew she wanted to say something about it. She knew it would be in her best interest to keep her mouth shut. She just walked away as I disciplined him. I couldn't believe she had the nerve to talk to me the way she did. I guess she forgot she was living in my house. The audacity of her to try and threaten me with my father was unreal. If it weren't for me he wouldn't have anything. They all should be grateful including Xiomara. I wonder how they would feel if I decided to cut them off. I loved the fact that I had my family around me. I went so many years without them. It just seems that now they are showing their true colors...green. In my opinion green is only flattering when it's folded in your wallet.

I checked the clock and it was a quarter pass eight. I flipped the covers off me and got out of bed. Enough was enough. I was going to get my husband. He hadn't called all day. I needed to make sure Aunt Rosa didn't drive him to the point of no return. I threw on a pair of shorts and a tank top. Lil' Jay was sleeping peacefully. I felt guilty for waking him up but I had to. I was not leaving him here with Aunt Rosa so she could have something else to throw in my face. I kept him in his pajamas and carried him to the truck.

We arrived at Mom Duncan's house twenty minutes later. I noticed Jay's truck parked in front of the house. The lights were off everywhere except the living room. I was relieved. Mom was sleep which meant I didn't have to worry about a lecture. Lil' Jay was still sleep. I removed him from his booster seat and carried him to the door. I know my shoulder was going to kill me in the morning, that little boy was solid and his head weighed a ton. I tapped on the door lightly. I didn't want to ring the doorbell. I didn't want to risk his parents waking up. A tapped a few more times and the door was finally answered. Jay opened the door with a smile and when he noticed it was me it dropped.

"What are you doing here?" His nose was slightly turned up and he didn't welcome me in. I ignored his rudeness and pushed pass him.

I laid my son on the couch and sat down next to him. Jay finally closed the door and followed me into the living room.

"Sasha why are you here?" He stood in front of me like he was waiting for me to get up and leave.

"Am I not welcomed here? Aren't my children here? The question is why aren't you home? Why haven't you called me all day?" I shot back at him.

He sighed deeply and sat down on the opposite couch. He rubbed the back of his head then put both of his hands over his face. I guess he was stressing. I went over to him and rubbed his back in attempt to make him feel at ease.

"Baby what's wrong? Is everything ok?"

He pulled away from me, "No everything is not ok...I don't know if it will ever be ok again." His last few words were a whisper. He didn't think I heard him but I did.

"What do you mean it will never be ok again?" My voice began to rise.

"Nothing-I didn't mean to say that. So much is happening right now. My job is taking a toll on me. Then there's this thing with you. I don't know what's going on with you. I leave for a few days and I come back your zoned out on pills. Azariah has turned into a disrespectful brat. Your Aunt Rosa

61

treats me like I don't belong in my own house. I'm beginning to think she's right. Maybe I just need to stay here with my parents for a while. I can keep my kids here half of the week and you or should I say Rosa can keep them the other half."

I was in awe. What I was hearing just couldn't be correct. Was my husband suggesting we be separated? My emotions where everywhere; I didn't know if I wanted to scream, cry or punch him. I was so confused. I didn't see this coming. Oh God! Was he seeing someone else? That's probably why he kept going away on these so called business trips.

"You son of a bitch! Who is she?" I jumped up and started pounding on him. "Who the fuck is she! Oh my God Jay why? Why are you doing this to us?" I screamed.

He tried to grab a hold of me and block my hits but I kept them coming. At this point Lil' Jay was screaming at the top of his lungs. Both of his parents were awoke and trying to get me off of him. Pastor Duncan was finally able to get a good grip on me and pulled me off of his son. Mom Duncan had a deep sadness in her eyes as she looked at me. I didn't care. I hated all of them. They were the enemy. How could she allow him to stay here? Why didn't she send him back home? They were church people didn't they know divorce was something like a sin? Jay stood before me with hurt and guilt in his eyes. I loved my husband I tried my best to do what was right. I broke down a wept. I cried so hard that I needed to vomit. Tears began to fall from his face.

"Sasha I-I never cheated on you. There is no other woman. There will never be another woman. I wish it were that easy. My family means everything to me and I don't want to lose it. That's why I decided that it may be better if we take some time apart so we can reflect on what we really need to do to make this work."

I wasn't trying to hear anything he had to say. It was all lies. If he loved us, well me, so much why would he leave? It just didn't make sense. I broke away from Pastor Duncan. All eyes were on me waiting to see what my next move would be. I couldn't stand being there any longer. I ran out of the house.

I hopped in the truck and pulled off. Halfway down the road I checked to see if he was following me. He wasn't and that hurt like hell.

I drove home like a bat out of hell; it's a wonder that I didn't get pulled over or worse get into an accident. I secretly wish something awful did happen that way Jay and his family would feel guilty. I unlocked my door and slammed it so hard I was sure the glass was going to break. I was on my way up the stairs until I was distracted by someone sobbing. I had every intention to ignore it. The only other person here was Aunt Rosa I figured she was doing her praying thing. She was always over emotional or as she would say in the spirit which would sometimes cause her to cry.

She began to get louder. I wasn't trying to hear that shit. I should be the only one crying; my family was falling apart whatever her issue was couldn't hold a straw to my problem. I busted in the family room ready to snap but the picture on the T.V caught my attention. My heart dropped to my stomach. The newswoman on CNN was speaking.

"The body of a twenty year old Arizona woman by the name of Starla Conner was found beaten and strangled in the dumpster at a nearby rest stop. The young woman's fiancé had filed a missing persons report on her two weeks earlier. As of now he is not a suspect in this horrible crime."

I was lost for words. I fell to my knees and screamed. Aunt Rosa ran to my side and held me. I couldn't stand another loss.

Chapter 14

Starla's funeral was going to be held in Burlington, New Jersey. The night I found out about her death I called Zachary he told me that she had a strange phone call and basically left the house. She never told him who it was. He said whoever it was really had her going. I asked him if she had heard from her mother. He said Camille had come to visit them several months ago. He said everything had been good between the two. He said he spoke to Camille when Starla went missing and she didn't seem too concerned. She just told him to give her space. I asked him were they having any issues. He said everything was fine as far as he knew and the wedding was still on. Starla didn't have any known enemies. The police had no leads it was like her attackers just targeted her and did what they had to do and were out. They wondered if it was a professional that murdered her.

I tried to call Jay when I found out however he didn't answer the phone. He didn't find out until the next morning when he came to pick up the children's things. I was still sitting in the den when he came in that morning. I was too numb to say anything. Aunt Rosa broke the news to him. For a moment he just stared into space while she was speaking. I knew that he had blamed her for Azariah's change. However she was still family and he used to treat her like his own niece.

"Do they have any leads on who did this?" He asked.

Aunt Rosa told him she didn't think they did.

He came over and rubbed my shoulders and gave me a kiss on the neck. He then walked out the room and continued gathering the children's things. He told me that he would call me later to check on me and that we would go to the funeral as a family. At this point I didn't even care. He showed no emotions and that made me sick. I didn't know who he was anymore. I didn't know who I was. Everything was going to shit rapidly.

We didn't tell Azariah about Starla's death until the day before the funeral. She cried for a short while. She then asked me if Starla was in heaven with her daddy. Xiomara and Aunt Rosa waited to hear my answer. I of course told her yes. What was I supposed to say, no your daddy is in hell. I guess they forgot she was only seven and too young to know what Lorenz put me through.

Jay stayed with us the night before we were to leave. He brought the children over. I was excited to see my babies. Lil' Jay was happy to be home as well. He gave Azariah a big hug when he saw her. She seemed to be happy as well. I made dinner that night and we laughed and joked like it was old times even under the grim circumstances. Jay and I slept together that night. We didn't do anything but we did cuddle. I was still angry with him but I had to admit it felt good to have his body next to mine. After the funeral I was going to suggest counseling. I needed my family back. I decided to do whatever was necessary to keep them. Even if it meant going along with Camille's plan.

Before we were off to the airport we dropped the twins and Lil' Jay back to Mom Duncan's. I wanted to protest but I decided to keep my thoughts to myself until we were back home. I didn't want to ruin things. Azariah went with us since Starla was something like her cousin. We flew into the Philadelphia Airport and checked into the Embassy Suites. Jehaida offered us to stay at the house. Jay wouldn't go for it. He told us we could go but he didn't want to be bothered. I didn't argue so I just let it go. There wasn't much room there anyway. She was living in my old house and with all of her children and new grandchild it would be cramped. I would have loved to see my sister and my nieces and nephews. I guess I would have to save it for another time. I was trying to sell her the house but she never got her credit straight enough to do it so I wanted to just give it to her, but Jay and Xiomara said she needed to learn responsibility.

The funeral was that evening. I had spoke to Camille a few times after the news came out about Starla. She seemed to be holding up well. I told her I would be there with my family. She wanted to know who I meant by family. I told her Jay was coming and his father wanted to come too. But he had to attend a conference and wouldn't be able to make it. She asked me if Starla was close to him. I told her how she had helped out in the church and Reverend Duncan had treated her as if she was one of his own. She seemed to be happy to hear that Starla had acquired an extended family

We arrived early and the sanctuary was almost at its capacity. Her Dad's family was there in full effect. We were seated with the family. We sat in the third row next to an elderly white woman. I spoke to her; she introduced herself as Starla's Great Aunt. I told her I was once her sister -in-law. I searched for Camille but didn't see her.

I saw Starla's father and I think the woman next to him was his wife. They were viewing her body. Jay leaned over and asked me if I wanted to go see. I told him no. Azariah wanted to go up; I didn't think it was a good idea, but Jay said she should so she can have closure. The two of them went up.

I opened the program and read the eulogy. I noticed that Greg's name was in there as her late father, beside her Biological Dad name. I shook my head, that Camille. I made a mental note to make sure Azariah didn't get to read it. I never told her about the brother on her father's side. I never saw a reason for it. I knew one day I would have to tell her something, especially now that Camille was back. Jay and Azariah made it back to their seat. I opened up the program so he could read it.

I leaned over and whispered. "I never knew Camille had siblings."

He was reading the program and a strange look came upon his face. That's when I noticed Camille being walked down the aisle with a young man. He had to be at least twenty five. She had a black veil over her face and was dressed in black from head to toe. Admittedly, she was sharply dressed as usual. I just wasn't feeling the veil.

Jay's eyes got big, he whispered."Is that who I think it is?" I nodded.

She leaned over the casket and wept, "Oh my baby who did this to you oh...God, you should have taken me...Oh lawwwddd, I know I've done wrong, but why take... my....baby. Oh...Godd...My Greggy is gone, Lorenz and now my Starla...Oh...God why has thou forsaken me...."

I was too through with this chick, and so was everyone else. People began to whisper. Azariah had a confused look on her face.

"Who is that crazy lady?" she whispered.

She had never met Camille and I wasn't looking forward to the union either. The young man who was with her helped her away from the casket. Her knees buckled and she collapsed in his arms. He caught her perfectly. A little too perfect if you asked me. Camille was a drama queen and I'm sure this was one of her performances. People began to whisper and few even giggled. Starla's father's face turned beet red. I knew he was pissed that she was once again stealing the show. This was supposed to be about her daughter but it wouldn't be Camille if all the attention wasn't on her. A few male ushers lifted her up and carried her to the nurse's station.

I noticed that Jay had his eyes fixed on her the entire time. It wasn't a look of shock. He seemed to be angry. His action almost made me believe what Camille said about him helping her was true.

"Why don't you seem surprised as I am, about Camille?" I kept my focus on him waiting for an answer.

"I will be right back." He excused himself and left out of the sanctuary. I wanted to follow him but I was afraid of what I might witness. So like a coward I sat there and waited for his return.

Jay never came back into the service. After everything was over I immediately began my search for him. I was sure his sudden disappearance had everything to do with Camille. I tried to get to the vestibule before the crowd. I had no such luck. I decided to take Azariah to the dining hall for refreshments. I didn't want her to see me have to confront Jay anyway. It was not going to be pretty. I sat her close to the door so I would be able to keep an eye on her while I searched for Jay.

"Zar I need you to sit while I go find daddy. When the lady in the black and white comes tell her what you would like to eat. If you need me I will be right out there, ok?" I pointed out into the hallway so she could see that I wouldn't be far.

She scooted her chair up to the table and patiently waited for the hostess. I quickly hurried into the crowd of people to start my search. There were so many white people there it wouldn't be hard to spot Jay. It took about fifteen minutes before I finally saw him coming out of what seemed to be some type of conference room.

"Jay!" I shouted waving my hand to catch his attention. He wore a disgruntled expression.

"Get Zar I'm ready to get out of here." His tone was nasty.

"Where were you all that time? You missed the whole service." I inquired.

He took hold of my arm tightly. "Sasha go get your daughter it's time to go." He said through quenched teeth. He gave me a slight shove before letting me go.

Part of me wanted to challenge him but the fiery look in his eyes warned me to do otherwise. I took a deep breath as I tried to suppress my anger. I rushed to the dining hall to retrieve as he had said *my* child. My blood was boiling. I wanted so bad to tell him the truth so he could feel stupid.

However I don't know how he would take the news. The way he had been acting lately I wouldn't be surprised if he would take my life on the spot for my betrayal.

I stopped in my tracks in shock. I felt the vomit rush from my stomach and stop in the middle of my esophagus. Camille was sitting at the table with Azariah eating cake.

"What the fuck!"

I looked to the left and Jay was standing next to me with his face screwed.

"I told that bitch to stay away." He huffed.

He rudely bumped people as he made his way to the table. I followed behind him apologizing along the way. He yanked Azariah by her arm pulling her from the chair knocking her cake from the table. She squealed in pain causing everyone to direct their attention to us. It seemed as if the whole room got quiet. I ran over to Zar to check out her arm. I held her tightly shielding her away from Jay.

"I thought I told you to stay the fuck away from my family!" He snarled.

Camille rose to her feet with a sly grin on her face, "Technically she's not your family. The birth certificate says she's a Hayward. As in Lorenz Hayward who happens to be my deceased son. I am her legal grandmother, and I have a right to speak with my grandchild. Isn't that right Sasha?" She looked me in the eyes directly. The look she gave me was daring.

Jay's face turned beet red.

"If you don't stay away I will get a restraining order to keep you away!" He threatened.

She began to laugh hysterically, "James sweetie you can't do anything without your wife's consent. Believe me when I say Sasha will not allow you to do such nonsense. You of all people should know not to threaten me. Shit your lucky if I don't sue you for grandparent's rights. Besides you like you Mom-Mom Camille don't you?"

Azariah shook her head yes. She looked up at me and said.

"How come you didn't tell me I have a little brother from Daddy Lorenz?

I couldn't believe that Camille had told her.

"I don't-I didn't know about him." I lied.

I couldn't take much more. I grabbed her by the hand and headed towards the nearest exit. I had so many questions I wanted to ask concerning her and Jay. But Camille threw shit in the game by dragging my daughter into the mix. Something was definitely going on between them two and I was going to get answers.

Chapter 15

Jay flew like a bat out of hell to the hotel. He didn't say a word just kept his eyes on the road. We when arrived I opened the door to get out.

"What are you doing?" He said with an attitude.

"I'm getting out the car what do you think I'm doing?" I snapped.

"You can stay in here. I'll get our things and I will be back down."

"Jay what are you talking about our flight doesn't leave until tomorrow. I'm tired and I want to get out of these clothes," I complained.

"We are leaving today. We're driving home." He shut the door and went inside the hotel.

I was confused. Why the hell were we driving back to North Carolina? There was no way I was going to ride over thirteen hours in church clothes. I was about to get out and my phone rang.

"Hello?"

"Don't say anything just listen to what I'm about to say. I'm giving you three days to get things together with your family. On the third day there will be a plane ticket to Atlanta. We have two weeks to complete what needs to be done. Once you do me this favor. You will never hear from me again. I promise." The phone hung up.

71

I tried to call her back. The phone kept going to voicemail. I tried a few more times before I caught a glimpse of Jay followed by two bellhops. They were bringing our luggage to the car. Jay got back in the truck and peeled off.

"Jay what is going on? Why are you acting this way?" He turned the music up and ignored me. His nose flared and he was sweating as he drove recklessly on I-95.

We stopped for gas at a station just outside of Baltimore. I waited until Jay got out to pay for the gas before I called Camille. When he was out of sight; I walked around to the back of truck and called her. She picked up on the first ring.

"Camille what is going on between you and my husband? He's been acting weird since he saw you," I whispered.

"That's not what you need to worry about right now. Once we take care of Shelly I will tell you everything. If I were you I would just drop it before things get out of hand. I will see you in three days."

"Camille...wait! Don't hang-!"

I felt the phone being snatched from my hand. Jay stood behind me fuming. He took my phone and threw it in the street. He grabbed my wrist tightly and backed me into the truck.

"Don't move you sneaky bitch!"

He pumped the gas glaring at me the entire time. I was totally pissed. He was getting way out of hand and it was about to come to a stop. I had been abused before and I was not going to allow it to happen again.

"I swear to God if you ever put your hands on me again it's going to be a problem." I tried to sound threatening but he didn't pay me any mind. He pushed pass me and got into the truck. Once we were both inside I continued on.

"Are you fucking Camille? Is that why you represented-"

Before I could finish he had slapped me in the mouth. I was in total disbelief. I felt blood trickling down my lip. Flashbacks of Lorenz went through my mind. I was infuriated. I was not going to let this happen to me again. I punched him dead in his mouth .At this point Azariah started to scream. He

72

grabbed me by head and held it down in the seat and applied pressure.

"Stay the hell away from that woman. If I ever hear about you talking to her or even so much as breathe her name around me you'll be sorry! Do you understand?"

"Get off me! I can't breathe!"

He didn't let go. A few seconds later I heard him say.

"Ouch you bit me!"

He let go of me and went after Azariah. I began to punch and claw at him to stop him from harming my child. At this point the cashier came from the store on the phone.

I heard her yelling, "I'm calling 911...I'm calling 911!"

He pushed me off of him and peeled off out of the gas station. I climbed in the back with Azariah and held her.

She was crying, "Mommy...Mommy! Are you ok?"

I nodded my head as I held her in my arms.

"I hate you! I wish you were dead!" Jay didn't respond.

"Zar don't say that about your daddy. He didn't mean it ok. He's just upset about the funeral."

I tried to make excuses for him. I didn't want her to hate him. He was still my husband. I wasn't sure how long our marriage would survive after this. She looked at my eyes swollen from tears.

"He's not my father; Starla told me the truth! That's why he hated her so much! I saw my father at the funeral today!

"Azariah that's not possible your daddy Lorenz is dead. I explained to you before that when you were a baby he passed on. That's when Jay took over. Please don't ever say that again."

Jay didn't say a word. I know he had to be hurt from what she had said. I was in shock myself. I couldn't believe that Starla would tell her something like that. It's not like we didn't tell her the truth anyway.

A few hours later Zar and I had fallen asleep. I woke up because I thought I heard a child screaming. I jumped up and saw Azariah being dragged out of the car.

"Oh my God Jay stop!"

I attempted to climb out but as soon as my leg touched the cement a pain shot through my left leg. Jay had slammed the door on me paralyzing me instantaneously. I couldn't move. He took of his belt and spanked her. I watched him beat my child like she was a stranger. I banged on the back of the window screaming for him to stop. He swung her little body around as she struggled to break free from him. By the time he was finished she was limp and tired out. He pushed her into the back seat with me and pulled off without saying a word. I broke down when I looked at my child; she was in a daze and numb. I tried to hold her and she didn't respond. I hated him. At this point my marriage was over.

When we arrived home he grabbed our luggage and placed it in front of the door and jumped back in the truck. He sat there for a moment before speaking.

"Look Sasha, I…we need some time apart. I need to figure out what I want to do. I just don't know anymore."

I opened the door to step out. As soon as I applied pressure on my left leg a sharp pain darted up my leg. I cringed in pain. Azariah was asleep there was no way I would be able to carry her however I refused to ask him for help. I didn't want him to so much as breathe on her. I shook her gently to wake her up. She jumped up immediately. She had a wild look in her eyes. I was pissed. He had traumatized my child. She was going to need professional help to get through this.

"Shh…Baby it's ok. We are home now you're safe, no one is going to hurt you." I assured her.

She jumped out the car and ran to the door. Before I shut the door I turned to him.

"Take all the time you need. As a matter of fact you can just stay away. After what you did I could care less if I ever see you again." I hissed.

He didn't look my way he just started his truck. When I shut the door he peeled off.

Chapter 16

Azariah slept in the bed with me that night. Early the next morning I received a call from Jay's mom.

"My son needs to be with us for a while. He has lost his way and he needs to be restored."

Her voice was weak. She didn't sound like herself. She usually spoke with authority. Her conversation was short and very distant.

"He needs help. He needs help." She seemed close to tears.

"Are you ok?"

"I'm fine. I have to go. Take care of that little girl of mine, she's the victim in all of this. If people weren't being deceitful and selfish none of this would be happening. I pray that the right thing will be done so all of this will be over!" The phone went dead.

I was a little taken back by that comment. I asked her what she meant. I had the right mind to call her back, I just didn't have the energy to argue. Instead I called my Aunt Rosa to see if she could keep Azariah for a while. I told her that I needed to go away on business. She didn't hesitate to take her. I told her that I would have her things ready the next day.

As promised Aunt Rosa showed up bright an early the next day. She was surprised to see me hobbling around the house.

"Baby what happened to you?" She hurried to my aid.

"Nothing I slipped that's all. It's just a little swollen I'm fine." I tried to make her leave the subject alone.

She had a weird look on her face as if she didn't believe me.

"So where is this conference?" she asked.

"In California." I lied.

"California? Wow lucky you! I wish I was going with you," she laughed.

"It won't be for leisure this is business only, I wish I didn't have to go but it looks like I have no choice but to go." I murmured.

"Azariah is in her room waiting on you. I hate to rush you guys but I have so much to do to get ready for this trip. I was told about it at the last minute with us just coming back from the funeral.

"Oh how was the funeral?"

"It was a typical funeral a lot of crying. Her family was very nice." I wanted to get off of that subject quickly too.

"Was her mother there?" she asked with a funny look.

"Excuse me?" I had an instant attitude. "Why would Camille be there she is in jail...remember!" I snapped.
She jumped back. You could tell she was shocked by my response.

"Sorry, I just thought the prison would let her come to her daughter's funeral that's all."

"Well she wasn't there." I turned away from her and headed towards the stairs, "Make sure you lock the door when you leave."

Once they were gone I hurried and I got dressed. I ran to my office to see if anything was there for me. Just as Camille promised there was a package on my desk containing airline tickets. I went through my computer and cancelled all of my sessions for the next two weeks. I sent an email to my secretary to let her know she was officially on vacation. At this point she probably wondered if she would even have a job. My attendance at work was almost non-existent, I was sure to lose a few if not most of my clients. The thought of my business going downhill bothered me, but not enough to renege on my plans. I had to take care of this situation; there was no getting around it. I closed out my email and shut down the computer. I took a deep breath before closing the door. Life as I knew it was about to change. I just prayed that God would have mercy on my soul.

Chapter17

I sat on a bench outside of the airport waiting for Camille. My plane had landed two hours ago and she still hadn't arrived. I tried to contact her several times however I was only getting her voice mail. I called back home to check on Azariah. Aunt Rosa informed me that my dad had taken her out for the day. I knew that she would like that; she had a strong bond with my father and the fact that he somewhat spoiled her didn't hurt. I told her I would check in with her later after I was settled. I thought about calling Mom Duncan's so I could speak to my son but decided against it. I was still not feeling the last conversation we had. I was dealing with enough. I didn't feel the need to take on more issues. I would let things cool down for a few days before I would reach out again.

I heard a horn blowing then my name called out, "Miss Sasha!"

I looked up and Camille was waving her hand at me like a wild woman. I had to do a double take. Was this chick driving a Ford Focus? I grabbed my luggage and headed towards her car. She popped the trunk for my things. Once inside I noticed she wasn't looking like her usual self. Her hair was pulled back in a loose pony tail and she had on a pink sweat suit. It looked like something you would find at Wal-Mart.

"Damn Camille what you can't tell time now?" I rolled my eyes as I buckled my seat belt.

"So how did you manage to get away from your over protective husband and the crumb snatchers?" She asked as she moved onto the highway.

I guess she wasn't going to acknowledge that she was wrong for having me sit around for two hours. I decided not to even take it any farther she wasn't going to admit she was wrong anyway.

"Actually it wasn't that hard. I let them know I had a conference out of state and I would be gone for a few weeks. Zar is with my Aunt and father and my other kids are with their grandparents...and father."

She chuckled with sarcasm, "Why are the children separated? I thought they accepted the little girl as their own. It's not like she doesn't belong to them anyway."

"They do accept her. They love her as their own. For some odd reason Zar has been actin' funny with them. I wonder why?" I cut my eyes at her.

"Don't look at me like that. The funeral was the first time I laid eyes on that child since she was born. I will admit that I told her about her *brother and other side of the family.* I figured I would join along with you and play the game."

"My daughter life is not a game Camille!" I felt my body begin to tense and my teeth clench. She had no idea the damage she was causing.

"Oh but it is honey! You've made it that way by carrying on with this lie for years. You could have very well told that man the truth when I sent you those test results. But no someone wanted to be greedy. Ain't greed one of those seven deadly sins? I know the Great Reverend Duncan has to preach on that. Or is he one of those pastors who only preach what works for him." Her hands tightened around the steering wheel and her face was twisted.

"What's wrong with you?" She had me confused.

"Nothing. I guess I would have done the same thing if I were you. I doubt it very much if I could have walked away from all of that money. I tell you. You are one lucky bitch. You ended up getting it all; loving family, great kids, a career and a shit load of money. Then again money isn't everything. It can't buy you a clear conscience." She looked at me and smirked.

I was speechless. She had hit a nerve and I didn't have the energy to argue. There was no need to, especially when she was right.

Twenty minutes later we pulled into a sub-division in the Henry County. I was in awe the homes were lovely.

"Wow who lives out here? It must cost a fortune to stay here," I asked as I admired the beautiful landscape.

This had to be where the celebrities stayed. My house looked like a row home compared to these.

"Girl these houses cost no more than two hundred thousand. Welcome to Georgia honey the place where you can make pennies and live lavishly."

"Two-hundred thousand? Wow my house cost three times as much and looks nothing like this. Who lives here?"
We pulled off to the side near a wooded area.

"Pay attention." She pointed to the house that sat by itself on a slight hill. It was the biggest house I had seen so far on the block.

I sat back and watched the house in silence. Camille looked at her watch almost simultaneously A sinister grin appeared on her face. The door opened and a man who appeared to be in his mid -fifties strolled out dressed in a dashing navy blue suit. His salt and pepper hair didn't match his smooth butter pecan skin. His face had a youthful look. His stride was charismatic. Handsome was an understatement. His whole demeanor had wealth written all over it. I looked over at Camille I noticed her leg was shaking uncontrollably. Her eyes were glued on him. That only meant one thing, either she had plans on getting with him or she already had.

"Who is that?" I asked.

"You tell me. Hurry look!"

I directed my attention back and my jaw hit the floor. "Oh my God! Is that-?'

"Yes ma'am, yes it is that trifling deceitful bitch!" Camille's frown was now upside down when she saw none other than her former lover and best friend Koshell or should I say Shelly following behind him. She pretty much looked the same besides the fact that she added on a few extra pounds. Her hair was still styled in the same luxurious blonde weave that flowed down her back.

"I can't believe that she actually looks good." I almost vomited when the words came from my mouth.

A sour look appeared on my face as I scowled and threw myself back in my seat. I couldn't believe I was acting so childish.

"I see you have a touch of that green eyed monster." Camille looked at me with mischief in her eye.

"Now you see why I'm so angry. This whore almost cost me my life and she's sitting here living it up. It's not fair. She doesn't deserve to be able to go on with her life as if nothing ever happened. She has to pay. Pay with her life." She squinted her eyes and her nostrils flared.

I know how she was feeling. Shelly played all of us. Her crafty and conniving ways made me lose my husband. The fact that her child was his never sat well with me. I was enjoying the wealth but I secretly wished that Azariah was indeed Lorenz's; things would have been so much easier if it was. Things weren't panning out the way I planned The last few years had been great but ever since her birthday things had went from sugar to shit.

"I hate to say it but I hate that she looks happy. She doesn't deserve this." I said in agreement.

"So that's why we are going to end it Miss Sasha." She started the car and pulled off

***

The front door to the house opened unexpectedly. I checked if I had any phone messages. There were none. My dad had stopped by a few days later. We didn't see him much. He had opened up a barber shop at our strip mall in Charlotte and had a new woman in his life, Ms. Linda. She was around his age, and was real sweet, but thought she was young. She kept herself up like the young girls. The kids loved her. He stopped by for a few hours and asked where the kids were. I told him Zar was in her room and Lil' Jay was staying at Mom Duncan's for a few days. He went upstairs to see Zar. Less than five minutes later, he was back down stairs with a vexed look on his face.

"What's wrong Dad?" I asked. He put both his hands over his head.

"Sash, why did my grandchild just tell me...that she didn't want me in her room because I was a killer." he said in a hurt voice.

"Oh my God! Dad, I didn't tell her anything...I swear" I stood up to go upstairs to find out where she got that from. He stopped me before I got to the steps.

"It's ok. She was going to find out one day. I'm a get ready to go. Tell her I love her...." he said.

I tried to get him to stay but he left out. Aunt Rosa had overheard everything. She walked over to me.

"I didn't want to say anything, but Azariah has been acting funny towards, everyone...including the twins...she says they're not her brother and sister really. She doesn't talk to me or Xiomara...we thought this is the way she is dealing with Starla's death. " She said.

I was fuming; she had no right to treat people this way. I told Aunt Rosa I would have a talk with her. I went to her room and she was on her computer.

"Azariah Becca Hayward...What is your problem! I yelled why did you say mean things to your poppi? Azariah kept typing on the computer like she didn't hear me. I snatched the keyboard from her and looked at the screen. She was using yahoo instant messenger. She was typing to someone with the screen name 'id agh711'. Before I could read anything she clicked the screen off.

"Who was that" I asked

She got up an unplugged her computer and got in her bed.

"Azariah! I'm talking to you! She continued to ignore me, Who...were...you...chatting...with?" Still no answer. "You know Zar...I can play that game too...if you don't tell me what's going on with you...you won't be in that play."

She put the pillow over head to avoid my voice. I wanted to knock her head off. I had to walk away before I did something I regretted. I opened the door to leave. I turned back and shouted.

"That's ok, be that way. I just hope you enjoy your summer up here in this room!"

***

Today was the Fourth of July and everything was out of whack. We would usually have a big bar-b que here at the house. But this year we were all going to Chuck & Xiomara's. I guess everyone knew there was some tension between Jay and I. The kids and I got dressed and went over their house. Azariah didn't want to go but she had no choice. When we pulled up I saw Jay's truck. I wasn't sure if I wanted to get out not. But I had too; Lil' Jay was running to my van. I opened my door and he jumped on me.

"Mommy...I miss you so much!"He said. I hadn't seen him in over a week. He wanted to go to Mom Duncan's with his dad.

"I miss you too, baby" I said. I kissed him on the cheek.

He jumped down and finished playing with his cousins. Jay walked over to me and gave me a hug. Sighing to myself because I truly did miss him. He looked at Azariah and she rolled her eyes. He took the twins from the van and carried them for everyone to see. Azariah sat in the van and played her Nintendo DS.I guess she wasn't getting out. I rolled the windows down for her and left her there. I didn't feel like arguing.

Everyone was eating and drinking. Jay's frat brothers were showing off doing steps. I went over to the table to fix me a plate. I thought about Azariah.

I wish she would just stop acting so stubborn and tell me what's wrong.

I made a plate for her and brought it to the van. She thanked me and continued playing her game. Xiomara asked what was wrong. I told her she was still going through it over Starla. She looked at me like I was lying. She didn't say anything and just walked away.

Chuck announced that they were going to set off fireworks so all the kids came running towards him. Lil' Jay ran and told Azariah. She came along with him to see the display. Jay and I were holding hands watching it. I guess that was his way of making up. He leaned up against me and I noticed his phone was vibrating. He picked it up.

"Hey dad" he said. "Oh..No..I'm on my way!" he ran over to Xiomara and said something to her.

I saw her grab her chest and put her hand over her mouth. He ran to me and told me to come with him. I asked him what was wrong. He told me they found his mother unconscious lying on the ground outside the church.

Chapter 18

For the last week Camille and I had been trailing Shelly and her family. The third day I was finally able to get a good look at Lorenz's son. He was a splitting image of him. He had the same bushy brows and defined facial features. My heart melted when I laid eyes on him. We were in the food court of Lenox Mall in downtown Atlanta. Him and his nanny were seated a few tables away from me. I was alone on this mission. Camille had disappeared as usual. We were staying at a hotel off of Peachtree. Most of the time, I found myself alone as she would dip off late at night and wouldn't return until late the next afternoon. I never questioned what she was doing. If I knew Camille as well as I thought I did she was off doing what she did best laying on her back.

This was one of those days that she was missing in action. This time she had left the car behind. I was tired of being cooped up in the room. So I decided to do a little site seeing.

However when I got into the car my plans changed, twenty minutes later I found myself sitting outside of Shelly's mini-mansion. I had no idea why I was there. I kind of felt silly. Just as I was about to pull off I noticed a little boy coming out the door. I felt an uneasy feeling overcome me. He stood by a silver station wagon. I placed my hand on the door handle, a part of me wanted to get out getting a closer look. However I knew that wouldn't be wise. So I started the car and drove closer to the house. I tried to get a good look but his head was down. I looked in the review mirror and noticed an older woman dressed in a blue uniform dress locking the door. I pulled into an empty drive way and waited for them to depart. I waited for a few moments then followed behind them all the way to the mall. I stayed a few cars behind them but made sure they stayed in my eye sight. When they parked the car, I made sure I got a spot in the same row a few spots away from them. I know what I was doing was insane, but I had to get a closer look. I was drawn to him like a fly to shit.

My phone rang and I noticed it was my dad's cell phone. I sent him straight to voicemail. I was busy, I would call him later. That's when I noticed they were heading to the food court. They were headed to Taco Bell so I grabbed something to eat at the Subway. Once they were seated I found a seat far enough to remain unnoticed but close enough to get a good look at him.

I fought back tears as I watched him. Memories of Lorenz flooded my mind. I even began to wonder what our child would have looked like. I couldn't fight it any longer I had to come to grips that I truly envied Shelly for having a piece of Lorenz, something that I would never possess. The nanny got up and went back in the line leaving him alone. Without thinking I got up and went over to him. I stood there staring at him as he played a game on his hand held gaming system. It took him a minute before he noticed me standing in front of him.

That's when I noticed his eyes. They were big and brown with amber specs throughout them. He was absolutely gorgeous. A warm welcoming smile spread across his face.

"Hello." He said cheerfully.

His voice was friendly. I felt a huge lump in my throat blocking me from speaking. I began to tremble.
His smile disappeared and a look of concern took over.

"Ma'am, are you okay?" He had a southern twank.

I managed to say. "Yes-yes I'm sorry I'm fine. You just remind me of someone I really miss."

"Well maybe you should call him. That's what I do when I miss my parents. I call them. Then I feel much better." He smiled.

I wish it was that easy. What he didn't know was that the only way I would ever be able to reach him would be in my dreams or death.

"Yeah maybe I'll do that. It was nice to meet you..." I waited for him to say his name. I just knew he was going to say Lorenz.

"Alonzo."

"Oh Alonzo...that's a nice name." I was shocked I was sure she would name him after his father. But Alonzo was close enough.

"Well Alonzo I have to get going. It was nice meeting you enjoy your day."

I hurried out the nearest exit. As soon as I burst through the doors, I burst into tears. My car was on the other side of the parking lot but I didn't care. I needed this time to let everything out. I was beyond hurt. That sweet little one was supposed to be mine, me and my Lorenz's child. Part of me wanted to run back in there and snatch him up. My phone was ringing again. It was Camille.

"Hello!"

"Where the hell are you? I know you didn't leave!" She screamed.

I began to cry heavy.

"Sasha...are you crying? What happened what's wrong?" she asked.

"I saw him! I saw him!"

"You saw who? Who did you see!" She said calmly.

"Alonzo, his name is Alonzo. Lorenz's son. I followed him and his nanny to the mall. He spoke to me Camille. He spoke to me. It's not fair. He was supposed to be ours. That was supposed to be my child with him. She doesn't deserve him! Oh God..." I bent over the hood of the car to catch my breath as my body convulsed from crying so hard.

"It's ok Miss Sasha. Don't cry. We will take care of it tomorrow. After tomorrow you will know longer have to worry about it. Now come on back to the hotel so you can rest. We have a lot to discuss."

She hung up the phone. I opened the car door and got in. I sat there for a moment before pulling off. If I wasn't sure before, I was sure now that I was doing the right thing.

Chapter 19

That night Camille and I stayed up late planning out our mission. She had everything mapped out. What she didn't know was that I had a plan of my own. Shelly's husband was leaving to go to a church revival in Baltimore, Maryland. Tomorrow was Thursday, from Camille's observations, she knew Shelly didn't go anywhere at all on Thursday. Why? We had no idea. The nanny left out every morning with Alonzo and didn't come back until late in the afternoon. That would give us plenty of time to handle our business and be out before anyone noticed.

Today was the day and we were walking around the bend towards the house. We wore dark jogging outfits to blend in with the other neighbors. It was about six in the morning, a little more than twenty minutes before the house would be clear. There was a trail in the back of their house that led to a wooded park. We jogged back there and waited for a while.

You could see their driveway from the park if you peeked through the bushes. I sat on a bench that gave me enough view to see when they were leaving. I sat in silence as I watched Camille jog back and forth. She had a determined look on her face. She was mumbling to herself. I guess she was hyping herself up for the moment. I didn't need to get hype. Yesterday's event was enough for me to do what I needed to do without a problem. I heard the engine start up. I hopped of the bench and peaked through the bush.

"They're leaving!" Excitement could be heard in my voice.

She ran over and looked. We watched as they backed out of the driveway.

"You ready to do this?" She asked.

I placed the hood over my head and began to jog down the path towards the house. I didn't need to tell her, she already knew I was ready. She followed behind me until we reached the house. I was about to go to the front door but she stopped me.

"Wait come back here." She went to the back of the house and I followed. She went to the backdoor and turned the knob.

"What are you doing?"

"What does it look like? Come on and be quiet I don't want her to hear us."

She pushed the door open slightly. She looked to make sure no one was there before she opened it any wider. Once she noticed no one was in sight she slid through. I followed closely behind her. She slowly closed the door behind us. I admired the huge Chef's kitchen that I was now standing in. I was in awe again. This place was a Chef's heaven. Everything was top of the line from the marble flooring to the granite and mosaic glass backsplash. I felt my arm being pulled. I didn't want to leave the space.

"Girl come on we got shit to do!" she whispered. She went towards a door off to the left. She opened it and there was a staircase.

I stopped in my tracks. Something wasn't right. How in the hell did she know the door was going to be unlocked and how in hell did she know there were steps behind this door. Where was the security system? There was no way for a place to be this plush and not have security.

"Come the fuck on!" she hissed.

I followed behind her. I placed my hand in my pants pocket to make sure everything was still there. We slowly made our way up to the steps. Once we were at the top I noticed we were in what seemed to be a closet. A huge walk in closet at that. All types of designer dresses and shoes lined the walls. I shook my head in disgust as we walked through. We stopped at another door that was slightly open. She waved me over so I could have a look. There she was laying on her huge king sized bed surrounded by pillows. Her back was turned away from us.

Camille pulled a handgun from the inside of her hoodie. She reached in her pocket and attached a silencer, then handed the gun to me. I didn't understand why she was giving it to me.

"What? I didn't say I was going to shoot her." I whispered.

"Bitch yes you are. Don't try to change up now. We had a deal." She said shoving gun in my hand.

"Camille I can't do this. She's not even aware of what's going on. Don't you at least want to confront her?"

She thought about it for a minute.

"You know what I do have something to say." She burst through the door causing her to jump out the bed.

"Oh my God who's there!" she screamed.

"Camille removed the hood from her head and shook her hair until it flowed freely. I rolled my eyes.

Did this chick just do that? She was such a drama queen.

"Oh my God! Camille is that you?" she asked in shock.

"Who else would it be sweetie? I brought company along too. Say Hello to Shelly Miss Sasha." I walked up and removed my hood. I didn't say a word I just stood there holding the gun tightly in my hand. The look on her face was priceless when she saw me. All the color drained from her face.

"Me-Me...I thought-I thought you had an accident. I don't understand. How-how are you here? I thought they sent you to jail." She looked back and forth at us as she tried to gather her words. Her body was trembling.

Camille walked over towards her. As she got closer Shelly began to back up. She was so shook up she didn't realize she was backing herself into a corner.

"I don't think what happened to me was an accident. As a matter of fact, if I remember correctly, you were the cause of what happened to me. You, my best friend, the one I shared everything with including my husband, betrayed me. Then you left me for dead. You never checked to see if I was ok. Do you know how much pain and turmoil I went through? Do you know how it feels to have your face smashed in glass and kicked repeatedly like a dog in the street? Do you know how it feels to see your flesh falling from your face or to go through a series of corrective surgeries? Do you?"

She was now standing directly in her face. Tears streamed down her cheeks. That was the first time I had seen Camille cry. I kind of felt bad for her.

Shelly broke down and cried. "I'm so sorry Me-Me. I'm so sorry. I asked the Lord to forgive me for what I've done so many times. I was ashamed for what I've done. I was sick back then. I was lost. We were both lost. We lived a wild and sinful life. I prayed that I would be able to see you again to make things right. I've changed. I found Jesus and he saved me Me-Me. I have a beautiful son. He looks just like Renzo. He's so sweet. You would love him. I told him all about you and Greg and his daddy. I want you to meet him." She wrapped her arms around Camille. "We make can make this right. I missed you so much."

I couldn't take it any longer, "Shut the fuck up with that fake bull shit!"

She turned towards me, "Sasha, I want you to know that I forgive you. God blessed my son and me with a wonderful man who is now his father and my husband. I didn't need that blood money. I hope that you have made peace with God and told that man the truth about your little girl. It's just not right…."

I had had enough. I raised the gun pointing it to her head.

"I'm not trying to hear that. Maybe you can sway Camille with your holier than though act but I see right through you. I can't believe that you have the nerve to say you forgive me. You should be asking for my forgiveness. You seduced my husband, shacked up with him, condoned his abusive behavior then had the nerve to lay up and get pregnant by him and have his baby! Are you fucking serious! He was my husband Shelly. I was his wife! I was his wife, not you! You had no right!" You are nothing but a whore and always will be. You deserve everything you get coming to you!" My chest was heaving and my hands were getting clammy. I was about to have another attack. I tried to control my breathing before I passed out.

Camille noticed what was happening she broke away from Shelly to help me as soon as she did. Shelly ran towards her door. I was on it. I ran too and tackled her to the floor. She attempted to grab me before she got the chance I pulled the syringe from my pocket and shoved it into her neck. She screamed out.

"Help! Somebody help me within seconds her body began to go limp. What's happening? I can't feel my legs. My body is burning what did you give me?" She slurred.

I pushed her off of me. I stood and began to drag her to her bed.

"Camille I need you to help me left her." She continued standing there watching.

"What did you just give her? Why does she look like that?"

"Fentanyl, it's a form of anesthesia. She has no use of any of her muscles. She can't blink, speak, nothing but breath. The dosage I gave her is enough to sustain a horse."

"Is that going to kill her?" she asked confused.

"Well I'm not sure, but too much of anything can kill you." I joked.

I was finally able to roll her in the bed. No thanks to Camille. I stood back and looked at her. She looked really creepy lying there stiff as a bored with her eyes not moving.

"Now what?" she asked.

I walked away from the bed and stood beside her.

"I don't know I thought you had everything planned out."

We both stared at her looking dumbfounded. Camille scanned the room as if she was looking for something.

"That's it." She walked over to the corner of the room. An iron was sitting on top of the bureau. She picked up and smiled.

"What are you going to do burn her with the iron to death?" I shook my head.

"This is an old school Black and Decker, it's old. You know what that means right?" she said as she plugged it in.

"What does it mean?"

"There is no safety on it. It's a fire hazard."

She turned the iron on high and sat it flat down onto the plush carpet. We both waited a few minutes to see if it was going to work. Minutes later you could smell the burning of the carpet.

"I think we are done." Camille said with satisfaction. She took one last look at Shelly before turning away. "What a waste."

She entered the same closet that we came out of. I quickly searched the area where I had fallen to make sure I didn't leave anything behind to link me there. Smoke began to rise from the carpet and that was my cue to go. I hurried out the room following Camille down the steps. Before we reached the bottom I wrapped my arm around her neck from behind causing her to fall into my chest as I choked her. She tried to grab my arm but her arms dropped to the side. The fluid released from the needle was already taking effect in her system. She collapsed in my arms. I let her body rest on the steps so I can get up.

I stood over top of her and began to laugh; her eyes were bucked staring at me. She tried to move her lips but nothing came out, no sound escaped.

"Sorry Camille but there was no way I was going to let you tear up my family. I have been through too much as it is. Besides you're no better than your girlfriend upstairs. Hopefully you two can be together again in the afterlife."

I ran out the house quickly. I ran all the way to the car not looking back. My past was finally behind me.

Chapter 20

The next morning I was on a flight back to Raleigh, North Carolina. I couldn't wait to get home to be with my family. The house fire was all over the news when I woke up in the morning. I didn't wait to hear what they had to say. The picture of the torched house was enough for me. There was no way that they could have escaped.

Two hours later I was pulling up to my front door. I was shocked to see Jay's truck in the drive way. I pulled up behind him and got out the car. I tried the door and it was unlocked. I went in and didn't see him at first. On my way up the steps I noticed he was sitting at the breakfast bar just staring into space. I came back down the steps and went into the kitchen.

"Hey, what's up?" I asked nonchalantly.

I opened up the fridge and acted as if I was looking for something.

"How was California?" He asked. I grabbed a bottle of water and shut the door. He was staring at me with a smug look on his face.

"It was ok." I opened the bottle and took a drink.

"Just ok?"

"Yeah ok. I mean I was working how was it supposed to be. It's not like I went shopping or site seeing."

"Well I figured you had to be having a great time. You've been gone for over a week and a half. I hadn't received a call from you. I tried to call your office to speak with Gazelle, of course there was no answer. So I go by there and your office is closed. What's going on Sasha?"

I slammed the water on the counter. This is not what I expected to come home to. Did he realize that I just committed myself to an eternity of damnation to save my family? I tried to walk away from him and he grabbed me. Oh hell no we were not gonna go through this bull shit again. I tried to snatch away from him.

"Get off of me!" I yelled.

He didn't let go, he held onto me tighter. The more I tried to fight him the tighter he held me. I was tiring myself out so I just stopped. I was tired of fighting. I let out a loud scream and began to weep. He hugged me tightly.

"I'm so tired Jay. I don't want to keep doing this. I love you. I want us to work out. But I can't keep fighting to make you stay. I've done all that I can and I can't keep going through this. I just want us to be like we used to be."

I buried my face in his chest and let all of my emotions that I'd been harboring for months out. He didn't say a word at first. He just held me in his arms and rubbed my back. After a few minutes he lifted me off him and looked me in the eyes.

"I don't want to lose you either. I love you. I can't see myself going on without you in my life. But something has got to give. I can't continue to live in this house and act like it doesn't bother me." His tone was soft yet firm.

"What are you trying to say?" I didn't know where he was going with this. *Was he leaving me*? I know just a little over a week ago I had vowed to never deal with him again. But after the events that took place in Atlanta. I knew I needed him and my family more than ever. There was nothing or no one else left to cause harm to us. I had made sure of it.

He let go of me completely and went to the kitchen table and pulled out a chair. He directed me to sit. Once I was seated he sat in the seat next to me.

"Babe, I don't know if you realize it or not but I made a lot of sacrifices to be with you. I allowed myself to be ok with raising a child that is not mine."

My face twisted when he said that. Before I could say anything he cut me off.

"Wait, let me finish. I don't regret it. I appreciate you for letting me take on that role of her father. I love that child with all my heart. Sometimes I forget that she's not mine. My family loves her. However, I can't tolerate your family or her *other* family filling her head up with who knows what and she disrespecting me. It killed me that I hit her the way I did. But those words 'He's not my dad' was like a stab to my heart. I was there when you were carrying her in your womb. I was there when she was born into this world. I was there for her first shot, her first tooth, the first time she spoke she called me da-da! I was her hero. Then she gets up with Starla and Camille and it's like I'm not shit!"

The tears that appeared in the corner of his eyes made my heart crumble to pieces. I had no idea he was feeling that way. I reached for his hand but he pulled away.

"Then it's this house. I can't live in another man's home that he built for my wife. It's a bruise to my manhood knowing that I am living off another man. Why don't you just sell the house and the businesses and put it in a trust fund for Azariah. This was left for her anyway not you."

I heard everything he said but it wasn't quite registering to me. *Why would I sell this house?* Greg had this built for me and Azariah. I was starting to think it wasn't so much about his ego being bruised but more about being envious. I decided to see where his head was at.

"I hear what you are saying and I understand that this may be hard for you. But you knew what you were getting into when you married me. Besides if I sold everything what would happen to my family? My father runs those businesses he depends on that income. Xiomara is in charge of the properties. *If* I sold this house. Where would we live...with your parents?"

He shook his head and pounded his fist on the table, "See that's what I'm talking about. You are so selfish when it comes to me! I'm your husband. In the bible it says we are supposed to be one. Nothing and no one is supposed to come before me. I'm supposed to be the head of this family so if I wanted to move with my parents you are supposed to follow. No questions asked!" He yelled.

Part of me wanted to get with him. I decided against it. Even though I didn't agree with him I was tired of the drama. Against my own will I said something that I prayed I wouldn't later regret.

"Alright I'll do it." I said softly.

He stopped in the middle of his ranting and emotional breakdown, "What?" he asked.

"I said Alright I will do it. I will put the house on the market sometime this week. I will talk to my family also and explain to them what is going on. I don't know how they are going to take it. Especially my father, I'm not sure if he's been putting any money up or anything. Xiomara I'm not so worried about. She'll at least have Chuck to fall back on." I said shaking my head.

I knew this was not going to sit well with my family. It was going to open a whole new dramatic situation. I guess it was better to have issues with them instead of issues within my own home.

"Are you serious?"

I nodded my head.

A huge grin appeared on his face. A sickening feeling just overcame me. I hope he didn't just put on a show to get his way. He gave me a huge hug.

"Baby I'm so happy that you said that. There's something I need to show you." He practically ran out the room. A few seconds later he came back with a folder and digital camera in his hand. He put the folder in front of me and opened it. I was confused at what I was seeing.

"What is this?"

I continued to look through the documents. I sat back in my seat in disbelief.

Settlement papers? He bought a house without telling me. Was he serious?

"Jay-you bought a house? A house in Cary? How? When? Why? I just-I don't know what to say. This is so...."

"Wonderful! I know! Take a look at the pictures I took." He handed me the camera. As I looked through them he continued to talk.

"Look at the size of the rooms, aren't they big. The kids will all have their own rooms. You have room for a home office, and look at the water features in the back. This house has everything. You and the kids will be happy here. It's not too far from our jobs or the church. I already checked out the school system, it's awesome." He was cheesing ear to ear.

He had truly thought everything through. I looked at the date on the settlement papers. He had just went into settlement two days prior. Everything was happening so fast. I didn't know how to react. I was angry because he had already purchased the house. So it didn't matter what I said. It was already a done deal. I guess if I didn't agree he was going to move on without me. That didn't sit too well with me.

I continued to stroll through the pictures in silence while I gathered my thoughts. I had to admit the house was beautiful. It was a brand new property and did seem to be bigger than the place we were currently in. I guess I could learn to love it.

"So when were you planning to move?" I sat the camera down on the table and stared straight ahead. I wasn't ready to look at him because inside I was boiling. The notion that he would have left without me was a slap to the face.

"Well I hired a moving company this morning. I told them I would let them know when I was ready by early evening. I was thinking we could get started as early as tomorrow."

My neck jerked in his direction so quickly. I thought I had given myself whiplash, "The morning! Are fucking kidding me? Jay I just got back home. I haven't even unpacked from my trip let alone pack anything up in this house. Are you using your brain? That is not humanly possible. Really what the fuck is the rush!"

I couldn't hold it any longer. I know he was shocked at the vulgarity coming from my mouth as was I but you can only take but so much before exploding. These last few months had changed me into a completely different person. I didn't know who the hell I was anymore. His chest was rising and his eyes were squinting. I knew he was about to let me have it.

"You need to calm down. If you would have let me finish you would have known that the upstairs and most of the rooms down here are completely boxed up." He said calmly.

I threw my head back. He was hitting me with all types of blows. I gave up. There was nothing else more to talk about. I obviously didn't have a choice in the matter. I was itching to ask him what his plans would have been if I didn't agree to move. I was afraid of what he might have said. I was more afraid of what my reaction would have been. I shook my head in defeat. He had got that one.

Chapter 21

The next morning, the movers where at the house bright and early. Jay was downstairs packing the rest of the house. Since this was his bright idea I refused to have anything to do with it. As soon as I heard the trucks I got myself together to get out of there. I couldn't deal with it. On my way out Jay asked where I was going. I lied to him and told him I was going to a realtor to see about putting the house on the market. He paused for a moment. I thought he was about to say he had already taken care of that too. Shit he did everything else. I was really on my way to see my father and let him know what was going on. I knew he would just be thrilled to know I was taking everything from under him.

The drive to Charlotte was about a two and a half hour drive. Which I didn't mind I needed time to myself to think about what my life had become. I knew I was going to have to do a zillion good deeds to get God's forgiveness for what I had done in Atlanta. Then again I may have done Him a favor it's not like those two chicks were anywhere near saints. They had done nothing but cause destruction. I laughed to myself as I thought about Shelly saying she forgave me. She had a lot of nerve. All the stuff she did to me and she thought I owed her an apology. That chick had to be high off of something and it wasn't Jesus. Poor Camille she really thought I was stupid. There was no way I could trust her. She would have told Jay about Azariah or even worse turn me into the police and say I killed Shelly. The more I thought about it. I didn't murder anyone. They died by a fire Camille set. I merely paralyzed them for a few hours. It wasn't my fault that they didn't recover in time. I began to feel better about the situation. I convinced myself that I didn't do anything wrong. It was their time to go. That was God's doing not mine.

I pulled up to my father's house and noticed that there were no cars there. I hoped I didn't drive all the way up here for nothing. I should have called before I came but I didn't find it necessary because he was usually home in the mornings. I checked the time on my dashboard and it was just a little after nine. I pulled into the driveway in front of his townhouse. The grass was freshly cut and the flowers were groomed. The house was small and older but it had great curb appeal. I walked up to the door and rang the doorbell. I heard someone coming towards the door. I was relieved. Seconds later Aunt Rosa opened the door with an old fashioned dress on. She had an odd look on her face.

"What are you doing here?" She asked with a puzzled look.

I walked in past her, offended.

What did she mean what was I doing here.

"What do you mean why? What am I not welcome?" I dropped my bag on the table and went into the living room to take a seat.

"No not at all. It's just Mixxon left this morning to take Zar to her grandmothers." She said in defense.

"Why is he taking her to Mom Duncan's when she was supposed to stay here with you until I returned?" People were starting to get on my nerves. Why are they just taking it upon themselves to do what they want when I gave specific instructions?

"We tried to call you all last week but you wouldn't answer. I don't know what happened exactly but Mixxon had to spank Zar...."

"He did what!" I jumped up of the sofa and went to retrieve my bag. I know damn well he didn't put his hands on my child. I know that's his grandchild in all. No one was going to discipline her but myself or Jay and I really didn't want him touching her. I didn't believe in beatings. I wasn't hit as a child and I damn sure wasn't going to allow my child to be abused.

"Wait Sasha before you call your father I need to tell you something." She pleaded.

"Tell me what? What would possess him to hit her? You don't know what my child has been through lately. She's not a fucking punching bag!" I snapped.

Aunt Rosa had a concerned look on her face.

"Sasha what is going on with you? Here lately you have been really hateful. You're not yourself."

"There's nothing wrong with me. Obviously there's something wrong with you if you think its ok for a grown ass man to beat on a child. I don't know how you were brought up but it's barbaric to beat humans. That's not how things are solved. But that's ok. I got something for all of y'all. Just watch and see!"

I stormed out the house before she could say anything else. In a way I was happy that this happened it would make it much easier to break the news to my father that life as he knew it was about to change.

Chapter 22

My Aunt Rosa called my phone constantly. I sent her straight to voicemail. When she figured out I was ignoring her she must have called Xiomara because next thing you know she started ringing my phone. I ignored her the first several times too. When I was just about to my destination I finally answered.

"What!" I shouted.

"Whoa pump your breaks honey! Don't what me! What the hell did you do to my aunt? She called me crying talking about you being disrespectful." She spoke nastily.

I already knew she was about to be on some other stuff. I wasn't quite ready for it. I know I had picked up some balls lately but Ziomara was different. Arguing with her would turn into a fist fight.

"Mind your business this has nothing to do with you. For your information I didn't do anything to *our* aunt. My issue is with your father. Again it has nothing to do with you. Since you want to call me and talk nasty without having your facts straight. You can find yourself another job. Take this as your two weeks' notice. Your services are no longer needed."

I hung up on her. She called right back. I was happy that we were moving now. I just hoped Jay didn't tell them where. But I'm sure he did because he and Chuck were the best of friends. Just to make sure I decided to call Jay before she told

Chuck what was going on. I didn't want him to be in the dark. I dialed his number and he picked up on the first ring.

"Hey Babe did my sister or Chuck call you? I asked.

He sounded as if he was out of breath.

"Yeah Xiomara is on the other line now. She just called and she seems to be angry."

Oh shit.

"Look I just had to fire her. She called me cursing me out about something she knew nothing about. Aunt Rosa was upset because I didn't want to listen to her excuse for Mixxon hitting Zar. So I'm on my way to your mother's house now to confront him about it."

"Wait hold up. Sasha what the hell is going on? Mixx hit Zar? Why is Zar on the way to my mom's? Why didn't he just bring her home?"

"Jay I don't know apparently your mother told him to bring her there. I'm just as confused as you. I'm going up there to pick up my child. She's not here, then Aunt Rosa acts like I'm not supposed to be here."

"Wait you went to Charlotte? I thought you were going to a realtor's office to put the house on the market?'

Damn I was caught up. I was running off at the mouth so fast I forgot my damn lie.

"I-I was but I decided to get Zar first. I was still going but- "

He interrupted me, "Sasha just stop it where are you now?"

"I'm about ten minutes away from your mom's house."

"I'm on my way. Don't get out that car until I get there!" He slammed the phone.

"Shit, shit, Shit!" I threw my phone on the passenger seat.

Things were getting ready to get way out of control. I had to get to my father before Jay did. He is gonna want to know why I ignored my father's calls while I was away. That was going to raise more questioning that I had no answers for.

I arrived at the Duncan's home and my father's truck was there. Jay hadn't arrived so that was going to give me time to say what I had to say. Hopefully my dad would get pissed and leave before he could show up. The front door was open so I decided to just open the screen door and walk in. I walked through the small hallway and went to the left. They were exactly where I thought they would be, in the dining room.

She bought all of her company to the dining room when she had something to talk about. When I walked in both of their eyes went directly on me. Before I tore into my dad I had to do a double take on Mom. It had been a minute since I've seen her and she didn't look too good. It looked as if she lost some weight. I would be sure to ask her about it but first I had other business to take care of.

"You got a lot of nerve Sir! I entrust you with my child while I go across country for my job and you abuse her! How dare you!"

He stood up and Mom Duncan slowly rose to her feet.

"Little girl you better watch your tone. I'm still your father. Ain't nobody abuse that girl. I did spank her. I had every right to if you would have answered the phone when I called you for over a week. You would have known what she did and why I did what I had to do."

I backed up a little. My dad was a big man and not to mention a murderer.

"What... you didn't call me. Anyway what could she have done so bad that you a man as big as you are would but his hands on my frail child?"

"She spit on me and said I killed her father and grandmother and that I was going to burn in hell for it! Did you tell her that? I know I wasn't there for you as a child and I apologize. If it wasn't for your mother and that nigga Greg I wouldn't have snapped. Do you know how I felt when I found out that Greg's son was your husband and he was beating on you? Do you have any idea how I felt when I received that letter that you were sleeping with Greg and his son? That killed me Sasha but I never judged you. I still loved you because you were my child. I blamed myself if I had been there none of this would have happened."

I felt like someone had taken a bat to the back of my knees; I wanted to hit the floor and vomit at the same time. He knew...my father knew that I was sleeping with Greg. Now Mom Duncan had known. I began to panic. Did Xiomara and Aunt Rosa know too? I wanted to go hide under a rock.

"I don't know what you're talking about. I wasn't sleeping with Greg. I don't know who told you that. But it's a lie. It's a fucking lie!"

"Sasha watch your mouth in my home child. I won't have any of that in here. You need to sit down and listen, your father loves you. Azariah knows better than to behave that way. We taught her better."

The front door opened and I heard Jay's voice yelling my name through the house. I couldn't respond or move. My eyes were burning, my heart was about to jump out of my chest any minute. It felt like the walls were starting to close in on me. Sweat beaded on my forehead. I held onto the wall for support.

Jay walked in and stared at me then everybody else.

"What's going on?" he questioned.

"He's lying on me. He's trying to turn your mother against me. He's said bad things about Azariah. I know she didn't say that she couldn't have, she doesn't know anything. I never told her. I never told her!" I cried. It was killing me to turn on my father but he left me no choice. He was airing out my business with no shame. Who knows what else he knew. Jay hurried over to me.

"Mom what's wrong with my wife. What did y'all do to her? Look at her there is something wrong." He was upset. He wiped my forehead and sat in the chair. He grabbed a bottle of water from an opened case that was sitting on the floor. Mom Duncan shook her head.

"It's her demons. They have taken clear over her. She needs Jesus in a bad way. She is nothing but a lying deceitful wonder!"

My ears had to be deceiving me? I know Mom Duncan wasn't talking about me.

"Mom this is my wife you are talking about! What is wrong with you?" I was shocked but happy that Jay was defending me. I was sure he would have jumped on his mom's side.

"No son what is wrong with you? I don't know this woman. She had me fooled. Just like that woman fooled your father!"

"Mom stop!" he barked.

"I don't know why I didn't see it at the beginning. She's a liar! Ain't no truth in her. She doesn't know what the truth is. I don't want her in this house! I don't want her to raise my grandchildren,0 none of them. That's why they are staying here with us. Tell Jay tell her she can't have 'em back," her voice was trembling.

I was lost. What did she mean they were staying with her. Did she not know Jay had bought a house?

"Mom I'm sorry but that's not your call. My kids aren't staying here. They are coming home with us. I'm going to work things out with my wife. I can't abandon my family. Mixxon I'm sorry but you are no longer welcomed in our home. I refuse for anyone to upset my wife the way you have or treat my daughter like that."

"Man don't even do it to yourself. That's my daughter in case you forgot. You can't keep me away from her or my grandchild. You don't even have anything to do with this. You ain't no blood to either one of them." My dad snarled.

I can tell he was getting ready to explode you could see the throbbing vein on the left side of his head.

"Mixx save that family bullshit for someone who doesn't know any better. You and I both know what your interest is in Sasha and Azariah. Family bonding damn sure ain't it. Why don't you tell her how I had to pay you in order to contact her? Why don't you tell her the only reason you had Lorenz killed was because of what his father did to you. Sasha had nothing to do with it. Better yet tell her about how you are smoking up all of her money!"

109

Jay and my father were standing face to face staring each other down. My dad moved so close to him that their noses were touching. I was sure Jay would have backed off but to my surprise he was standing his ground. Jay wasn't a scrawny man standing six foot two and about two-hundred and twenty-five pounds, but still it wasn't nothing compared to my father. I continued to sit in the same place trying to make since of everything that was going down. I was at a total loss for words.

I heard Jay laugh out loud, "Yeah I didn't think you would have the balls to tell her." He turned to walk away and that's when it happened.

Mixxon grabbed him and put him in a headlock and started to choke him out. I started screaming for him to get off of him. They were tussling and fell into the table. Mom Duncan was standing in the corner crying and praying. I hurried to my feet and ran over to them. I grabbed my father and tried to get his arms from around my husband's neck. When I grabbed him he swung me off of him sending me crashing onto the floor. I got back up immediately. I looked around for something to hit him with. That was the only way I thought I was going to be able to stop him from killing my husband.

I spotted a brass candle holder on the table. I grabbed it and knocked my father on the side of the head twice with it. He flinched but didn't let go. I bit down on his arm causing him to loosen his grip. Jay managed to break out of his hold. That's when he started wailing on Mixx who was now shaking me like a rag doll. He pushed me hard this time. When I hit the wooden floors I wasn't getting right up. I landed hard on my side. Pain shot through my whole right side. I watched as they fell over the table and into the corner where Mom Duncan was standing. I saw what was about to happen and by time I could attempt to do anything about it, it was too late.

"MOM!" I yelled as I saw her body fall and her head bounce off the edge of the end table.

Mixxon's body had crashed into hers forcefully knocking her to the floor. Blood oozed from the side of her head onto the floor.

"Oh shit! Mom! Mom!" Jay screamed at the top of his lungs as he headed towards his mother. Mixxon got up from the floor quickly. He saw Mom Duncan lying on the ground. But it didn't faze him he was too far gone…nothing was going to stop him. I knew I was going to have to do something to stop him before someone ended up dead.

Chapter 23

I willed myself to get up from the floor. When I stood up I thought I was about to collapse again. Mixxon had gotten a hold of Jay again and was beating him senseless as Mom Duncan laid on the floor unconscious. The blood was rapidly spilling from her head. If something didn't happen fast there would be three dead bodies before this ordeal was over. I remembered that I still had a extra syringe filled with Fentanyl left in my bag. I was supposed to get rid of it but got around to it. I grabbed it out and flicked the cap off. I ran over and stabbed my father in the neck. Before I could pull it out he grabbed my arm. The look in his eyes was one of rage and shock. He didn't say a word he just stared at me before he dropped to the ground.

I ran over to Jay, his face was bloody. His jaw hung loosely and his eyes were beginning to swell.

"Oh my God baby I'm so sorry! I'm going to get help!"

The house phone was still in place on the table that Mom Duncan was next to. I called 911 and told them we had an emergency. When I hung up from the operator was when common sense kicked in. I just messed up majorly. I injected my father with the same substance I used on Camille and Shelly. He was still lying on the floor unable to move. I moved the needle from his neck.

What the hell am I going to do with this?

I noticed the flower pot on the opposite side of the room. I tried to push the syringe down in it but it was too dry. I could hear the sirens coming towards the house. I didn't have much time. I grabbed the water I was drinking off the table and threw it in the dirt. I forced the syringe deep inside. I heard doors close and people talking before I heard a loud knock followed by, "Police we are coming in!"

"In here. He's in here hurry!" I yelled.

Two state troopers came in with their guns drawn.

"Help me please! My father attacked my husband and mother in law! She's hurt badly," I cried.

"Ma'am what happened in here?" The officer asked while his partner called for back-up.

I explained to him my version of what happened leaving out the part of me stabbing him.

The medics came within minutes. They tried to check me but I refused. I wanted them to hurry and get my father out of there before he came to. They carried Mom Duncan and my father out first. When they came back in for Jay the female medic had a puzzled look on her face.

"Ma'am what exactly happened to your father?" she asked.

I sat silent for a moment to get my story together. The officer that I was speaking with waited for me to answer.

"I-I told you that he had attacked me and my husband tried to defend me. As you can see he's a much bigger man than my husband so he pretty much over powered him. I didn't know what to do. So I grabbed the candelabra and hit him with it a few times. Then he hit me again and I guess I blacked out for a minute because next thing I know my husband and his mother was on the floor and my father was just laying there. That's when I called you."

From the look on their faces I could tell they were finding my story hard to believe. If it was me I wouldn't believe it either, but I was lost. There was no way to explain why my father was in the state he was in.

"Does your father have any medical issues?" she asked.

113

"Not that I know of…but I just found out that he has a cocaine habit. Matter of fact that's what caused all the chaos today. We were doing an intervention and things got out of hand."

The look on both of their faces softened.

"Oh I'm sorry to hear that. That explains a lot. We are going to wake him medically unless you had another preference."

No that's fine. I have to get in touch with my father in-law he's at a church convention. I need to let him know what is going on with his wife."

I spoke with the officer for a few more moments before I called Rev. Duncan.

A half an hour later I sat in the room with Jay while his lip was being stitched up. The doctor said his jaw was fractured and not broke which was a good thing. Mom Duncan was another story. We all were in for a surprise when we were told that Mom had a tumor on her brain that was cancerous. This was not something that was just discovered. She had been aware of her condition for months and hadn't shared it with anyone. We weren't sure if her husband had known about it.

Her doctor explained to us that she had been in treatment the last six months and had recently stopped because there was nothing more they could do. The tumor was in an odd place and if they did surgery her chances of survival was slim. He informed us that the impact to her head from the fall had caused a blood vessel to burst in her brain. With the bleeding on her brain he doubted if she would be able to hold on for much longer.

Jay broke down in tears. Although his cries could not be heard his actions spoke volumes. His body convulsed and cringed as the anguish showed upon his face. He was in deep pain; not the pain that came from physical hurt but that of deep emotional hurt. I knew he was feeling some type of way. The last words that he had with his mother were not ones of love but filled with bitterness.

I was guilt ridden. I wanted so bad to feel his pain but I couldn't. My mind was on how I was going to deal with Xiomara and Aunt Rosa. I hadn't even called and let them know what was going on with Mixxon. I know they were going to be livid. All of this could have been prevented if I had just answered the phone when he called about Zar's behavior.

Oh my God Zar! Where the hell are my kids?

It had come to me that in the mist of all the action Zar or the rest of the kids were nowhere in sight.

"Jay where are the kids? Weren't they with your mother?"

"No its vacation bible school week. They at the church." He slurred.

"I was relieved." I forgot all about vacation school.

The nurse handed Jay his papers and we left out the room to go sit with his mother. I held his hand as we boarded the elevator. I squeezed it and he didn't respond. He was so numb and distant. Before the door could shut all the way a hand stopped it from closing.

"You fucking Bitch! You set my dad up! You crazy whore!" Xiomara was screaming like a banshee.

She grabbed my hair and started clawing at my face. I tried to defend myself by swinging at her. She was pulling me out of the elevator. It seemed like forever before Jay helped me. Security was there before he even decided to help. The guard grabbed a hold of Xiomara as she was going crazy.

"I swear to God imma kill you! If it's the last thing I do. You are going to pay for what you did!"

I didn't know what the hell she was talking about. There was no need for her to act this way. I couldn't wait until her and the rest of them were out of my life.

"Ma'am are you ok? Do you know this woman? He asked.

I wanted to curse him out but I decided against it. I had a working relationship with this hospital. I damn sure couldn't act a fool. It was bad enough that people saw me being attacked by my sister.

115

"Yes, I'm fine. I'm Dr. Sasha Duncan I would like her removed immediately She's my sister and I don't want to press any charges."

He was placing handcuffs on Xiomara.

"Dr. Duncan I understand but I still have to retain her until the authorities come. I witnessed her attack you. I'm also going to have to ask you to stick around to write me a statement."

I heard Jay sigh deeply. I was agitated because he hadn't done anything to defend me. I know he was going through it but I was just attacked in front of him and he hadn't done or said a thing about it.

"Jay you can go upstairs I need to take care of this. I'll be there in a minute."

He walked off without saying anything. I followed the guard to his office. Xiomara shouted obscenities in English and Spanish the entire time. Once we were in the office and out of site I let her have it.

"What the hell is wrong with you? Why are you embarrassing me and yourself like this? Do you realize that Mom Duncan is dying? "

She spit at me and it landed on my shoulder. The guard threatened her with the stun gun if she didn't calm down.

"Fuck you!" She said to him and then turned her attention to me. "We tried to be there for you and this is how you do us. Strip us from everything and send my father back to jail. They are charging him for attempted murder and assault and some other shit! I swear to God I didn't talk him into coming down here."

"I've done nothing but make your lives better. If it wasn't for me you would still be living in section eight housing living off of welfare and unemployment. Your father probably would have been dead or so strung out on coke that he was one of the living dead!" I snapped.

"What! Fuck you Sasha! Fuck you!" She tried to kick at me. The guard was fed up with her and shocked her with the

116

gun. Her body shook as she screamed. I turned my back and filled out my statement.

Chapter 24

I woke up the next day feeling like I had been in a car wreck. My head hurt from thinking too much and my body from being thrown around like I was nothing. It didn't help that I had slept on the hard floor. I sat up and looked around the unfamiliar room filled with boxes and my bed that had not been put together. The moving company had moved everything to our new home yesterday. They were going to come back today to unpack and set everything up but I called to reschedule due to everything that was going on.

Yesterday after my situation with Xiomara, I joined Jay as he sat with his mother and waited for his father and sister to arrive. After sitting in silence for hours, I couldn't take it anymore, I tried to talk to him but he was very short with me. I told him I was going to get the kids, again he didn't respond. So I left.

When I went to the church to get my children everyone was in the sanctuary praying. I figured Rev. Duncan had already informed them of her condition. I spotted my children immediately Lil' Jay was sitting on the pew playing his DSI as usual, Azariah was on her cell phone texting away. I saw two baby seats on the pew in front of them. My heart filled with joy. I hadn't seen my babies in a while. I hoped they didn't forget who I was. At that moment I felt to have four beautiful children. I had begun to wonder if all this lying and scheming was even worth it. They had come close to losing both of their parents yesterday. I don't know what would have happened to them if we were gone. I couldn't fathom the idea of them going with the Diaz's, especially since I now knew their true feelings about me.

Jay must had sensed my as soon as I started down the aisle he turned around and screamed "Mommy!"

He ran over to me and Azariah followed as well. They both gave me big hugs and told me how much they missed me. Before I knew it I had a crowd of people asking me how Mom Duncan was. I told them the bare minimum. I didn't know how much they knew. I excused myself and went over to my babies. I held them and kissed them. I couldn't wait to get them home until it dawned on me that we were in the middle of moving. I didn't have the proper place for them to sleep. I knew they would be disappointed. I explained to Sister Mille what was going on and she told me they could stay as long as I needed them to.

To my surprise this kids were ok with it too. I gave them kisses and told them I would be back to see them the next day. I called Jay to see what time he would be coming home. He didn't answer. I decided to just leave him alone I know he was going through a lot.

I slowly rose from the little pallet I had made on the floor consisting of a few blankets and a couple pillows. It would have made more sense to get an air mattress. I was too tired to stop at any stores. I looked down at my cell phone to see if anyone had called. There was only one call from a number I wasn't familiar with. I checked my text messages there were several from Xiomara. I just erased them. I could only imagine what they consisted of. I checked on the time and it was just a little after eleven. I couldn't believe I had slept that long. I really didn't understand why I hadn't heard from Jay. I decided to give him a call. I dialed his cell phone and again it went straight to voicemail.

Why is he being this way?

I shook my head and placed the phone on one of the boxes. I couldn't understand how at one point he could be so

119

sweet to me and within in minutes turn around and give me the cold shoulder. Then I had to realize that his mother was on her death bed. I had been there myself when mine had passed away. My circumstances where different though. I had time to prepare for my mother's death. This was so sudden for him. It didn't help that he had just chose me over her. Then got into a fist fight with my father which caused her to be in the condition she was in.

I prayed that he didn't have resentment towards me. That could be the reason why he was so distant. Just when I thought I had gained my husband back I could be losing him again. I refused to let that happen. I was going to be selfless and be there for him no matter what. I knew what I needed to do and that was to go to that hospital and be by my husband's side.

I arrived at the hospital forty-five minutes later. On my way up to the intensive care unit my phone rang. I noticed it was the same number that was on my missed call log.

"Hello Dr. Duncan speaking"

"Dr. Duncan?" It was a man and he seemed to be confused. Maybe he had the wrong number.

"Yes, this is Dr. Sasha Duncan...." I reiterated.

"Oh they didn't tell me you were a doctor."

I was now the one confused.

"Who's this?"

"I'm sorry this is Detective Mark Peters with the Wake County Police Department. I'm investigating the Diaz case. I wanted to ask you a few questions concerning the incident. Do you have time to come in or could I meet you somewhere?" He asked.

I couldn't see what more he needed to know I told them everything, "Well there is nothing much I can tell you. I told the officer everything. It's pretty self-explanatory. We had a family discussion that went bad and an innocent woman is now on her death bed due to my father's belligerent behavior." I said matter of factly.

"Dr. Duncan if you don't mind me asking, what field of medicine do you practice?" He asked suspiciously.

"I am a Behavioral Psychologist. I don't practice medicine per say." I didn't see where he was going with this. I hope he wasn't one of those people who didn't respect the field. "Why do you ask?"

"Well I received your father's lab work and he showed positive for Cocaine and Fentanyl. The cocaine is one thing but it riddles me on why and how Fentanyl would come up in his system. Are you familiar with this drug *Doctor*?"

I played it cool. I already knew what he was doing and I wasn't going to fall for it.

"Actually detective I'm sure I've come across it in my studies. As I already stated I'm not a medical doctor so I don't familiarize myself with drugs unless they are used in my field to treat the disorders that my patients deal with. I hate to be rude but I'm at the hospital with my husband whom was also attacked by my father. His mother is in a critical state."

"Well Dr. Duncan, I must tell you that this is the first time I've ever come across something like this. Fentanyl is an anesthetic and can also be used for a pain medication. This stuff is like ten times more potent than morphine. There is no way this guy could have shot himself with it and then get into a brawl without hitting the floor almost immediately. Someone had to inject him with this. Besides that an IV is the only way you can administer this drug. I know about your mother in-law that's a very sad situation. I tried to get in touch with your husband earlier I know this is a hard time for him. He's a nice guy and a hell of a lawyer. I saw him in action a few times. Listen…could you do me a favor and let him know that I need to talk to him as soon as possible. The sooner I speak to him the quicker I can close this case. In the meantime I'm going to head over to the county to speak with Mr. Diaz. Maybe he could tell me how he *managed* to get Fentanyl in his system. You have a wonderful day Dr. Duncan."

"You do the same Detective." I said with a fake smile on my face. As soon as he hung up I started to curse silently to myself. How the hell was I going to get out of this? I know my father was sure to tell him I injected him with something. How was I going to explain that? Then again I was safe, they had no evidence. It was his word against mine.

Chapter 25

A week had passed and Mom Duncan was still in a coma. We were now living comfortably in our new home. Jay and I along with his father and sister spent most of our time at the hospital. He was opening up to me more and more. He didn't talk about the incident. He basically talked about our future together. I was happy at the fact that he still wanted a future with me. His relationship with Zar was still a little shady. It was almost as if they were both avoiding one another. The affection they shared for one another was weak, almost to the level of fake. I didn't say much about it. They had been through a lot and I know healing took time. I hadn't heard back from the detective so I guess my father hadn't said anything about what I had done; which was great for me.

As far as the rest of my family, things where totally out of control. I had to get a restraining order for Xiomara. She would call my phone and threaten me daily. Her behavior had put a strain on Chuck and Jay's relationship. Chuck loved Jay like a brother but Xiomara was his wife so of course he sided with her. That hurt Jay deeply. He didn't say it but it showed. That his best friend since high school and now their friendship was over. I couldn't help but notice our relationship was causing us to lose everyone around us. I guess it didn't matter as long as we had each other.

It was Thursday evening and we were in the waiting area while Rev. Duncan was visiting with his wife. Jay and I were watching a game show on the television when his father ran out the room panicking.

"She's up! Thank you Jesus! She woke up. Jay and I jumped up and followed him into the room. I looked over at the bed and sure enough Mom Duncan was wide awake. Her big round eyes darted about the room in confusion. A nurse rushed passed me to her side.

"I'm going to need you guys to leave the room so we can check her. We'll be with you shortly."

We abided by the rules and went back into the hallway. Jay gave me a huge hug.

"You hear that baby. Mom is back! Our God has the last say!" He proclaimed.

I smiled back and agreed with him. Jay had been spending more time in prayer lately. He told me he believed his life was in disarray because he was not doing God's will. I couldn't argue with him because we had all fallen off track. I just hoped that I wasn't too far from redemption.

"Baby I'm so happy. The kids are going to be so excited." I said.

Rev. Duncan called Jay's sister who was home watching the kids. I could hear her scream through the phone. We waited for over an half an hour before the nurse gave us the ok to go in. I let Jay and his father go in first. I wasn't in a rush. I wasn't sure if she remembered anything that happened. I wasn't one of her favorite people and I didn't want my presence to upset her. About fifteen minutes later they both came out with huge smiles on their faces. Jay's face was stained with tears. To see him overjoyed brought tears to my own eyes.

"How is she? Can she speak?" I asked.

Jay laughed. "Can she speak? When was there a time when Mom couldn't get something said? How about you go and find out for yourself?"

I was a little hesitant.

"I don't know Jay. I mean I-I don't know what to say."

Rev. Duncan interjected.

"Baby take your tail in there and see your mother. Besides she asked to see you," He laughed.

"She asked for *me*? I was surprised.

"Yeah she did. It's ok. Everything is ok." Jay assured me.

I slowly went towards the room. When I arrived at the door I took a deep breath before going in. I went in and stood at the foot of the bed.

"Hi Mom I'm glad to see your awake." I said sheepishly. She tried to raise her head to talk but she was too weak. She motioned for me to come closer by the wave of her hand. I reluctantly moved to her side. This was first time that I can truly say I paid attention to the way she looked. Her body was filled with fluid causing her skin to look shiny. Tubes were running throughout her whole body. The only thing that was never in place was a breathing machine. I knew it had to be God to pull her through this.

"Hi mom." I said again.

She didn't say anything she kept staring at me. It seemed as if she was looking deep into my soul. It was freaking me out.

"Ok mom I'm not going to keep you, get your rest. I will be back to see you tomorrow." I turned away and I heard her say in almost a whisper.

"Tell him the truth."

I turned around quickly, "What did you say?"

"Tell him the truth it's the only way you'll be free...."

"I don't understand. What truth?"

"Tell him about his child Sasha. He needs to know. Don't make the same mistake his father did. It's a curse...tell 'em"

Her eyes began to get heavy as her voice trailed off. I looked around the room to make sure no one else had heard what she had said.

"Mom...mom...please wake up. Can you hear me? How did you know? Who told you?" I was in a panic.

How did she know about Azariah? What did she mean by making the mistake his father made. What did Rev. Duncan do?

I ran out and got the nurse. I needed her to wake up.

"I need help she was talking and she just stopped!" The nurse looked at the monitor.

"She's fine ma'am she's just sleeping."

"Sleep? Can you wake her up? She was telling me something...."

The nurse smiled, "No ma'am she needs her rest. You can come back and talk to her in the morning."

Unfortunately the morning never came for Mom Duncan she passed away later that evening. Taking all the answers to my questions with her to eternal glory.

Chapter 26

Mom Duncan's funeral was like no other that I experienced. There were no tears of sorrow or falling out in the aisle. It was more of a celebration. That's what they called it, a home going celebration. The entire C.O.G.I.C ministerial staff across the East Coast was in attendance. Choirs from far and near came to perform and show respect to a woman they described as meek and a mother to all. It was ordered that the family wear all white to celebrate her life. Rev. Duncan performed the service to my surprise and he did a wonderful job. Jay was in good spirits as well. He told me the night when we received the news that she had passed that he was ok with it. He had made his peace with her.

I couldn't say the same. I was actually bitter. Bitter because I felt that she died on purpose to taunt me. How could she just give me a few pieces to the puzzle that I could never complete? I had battled within my mind since that night. I had no idea how to take what she said. I couldn't very well ask Jay what the mistake was that his father made. He probably didn't know. Jay put his dad on a pedestal. Everybody including Mom Duncan made him seem like this perfect person. There was never a scandal attached to his name like some of these other preachers.

After the funeral we all met up at Mom Duncan's house. It felt funny to be in there since she wasn't there. The kids seemed not to be affected by it all. Zar and Lil' Jay knew that she was in Heaven with God and the Angels, and they were fine with it. I was sitting in the den feeding one of the twins when I heard my name called.

"Sasha can I talk with you." Aunt Rosa sat down in the chair in front of me. I didn't know what to say. She had been the only one I hadn't heard from since everything went down.

"I don't really think you should be here and I don't have anything to say to you." I said coldly.

"Sasha don't be rude. Mom Duncan was a good friend to me. I loved her like I would love my own mother. Sasha I don't understand what happened between the family. I just need you to know that I love you. I always will love you. I love my great nieces and nephews. I can't change what Mixxon has done. But he wasn't the only one at fault. This is your work too. If you had just listened maybe this would not have happened. Instead of gathering for a funeral we could have been here for a happier reason. I am here not only to pay my respects to my dear friend but to let you know that I'm going back to Delaware but before I left I wanted you to know that I will always be here for you. Your father wants to speak with you. He says there is something important that you need to know. So please go to him. It seemed urgent. Before I go is it alright for me to say good-bye to the children?"

I thought about it for a moment. She really didn't do anything wrong to me. I handed her the baby.

"Sure Aunt Rosa you can say good-bye to them. I need you to do a favor for me. Let that man know that I will never come to see him. He no longer exists to me."

She stared at me with great sadness. She kissed both of the babies and handed them back to me.

She gave me a hug and whispered in my ear, "If you want forgiveness you have to forgive others." Before walking away.

Later that night I lay in my bed restless. Jay was sound asleep snoring. I hopped out of bed and went downstairs to make a cup of sleepy time tea. I hoped that would do the trick. I had a bottle of Xanax in my purse I knew they would put me right to sleep. However I really didn't want to go down that road again. I was trying to do things right and popping pills would just add on to my problems. I sat at the table sipping on my tea in deep thought. My life had changed drastically over the last six months. I tried to pin point a certain time of when it was falling apart. If it was up to me I would have said things changed the day the delivery came. The truth is it changed the day I decided to live a lie.

The last words that Mom spoke to me haunted me daily. I tried to figure out how she knew. I just couldn't grasp the idea of her just *knowing*. I know she would say God spoke to her. *Did he really tell her? If so why didn't she tell Jay.*

I thought about how she treated Azariah when she was first born. She would always refer to her as her grandchild even before we were married. I thought about what Aunt Rosa said about forgiveness. I wasn't sure if I could ever forgive my father after knowing that he really had no interest in me. The things he said about me and Greg that day pierced my soul. I couldn't imagine what he really felt about me. Just the thought of it made me sick to the stomach. How much did he really know about my past I wondered. I guess the only way I would know is if I went to see him.

Chapter 27

Summer was just about over and the kids were on their way back to school. Little Jay was due to start kindergarten in a week and Azariah was on her way to second grade. It had been a little over a month since Mom Duncan had passed on and everything had finally gone back to normal. I had returned to work and Jay as well. His mysterious business trips were non-existent. He spent more time with us than he had in the last year. His relationship with Chuck had healed. So he was much happier. I couldn't say the same about Xiomara, she still held a grudge against us. I was told that she even gave Chuck an ultimatum; either her or Jay. He was at our house on a weekly basis watching the game with Jay so I guess that didn't work in her favor. We both dedicated our life back to God. So things had been great at home. His relationship with Zar had even improved. It wasn't quite where it used to be but at least they did interact. I believed that in time they would be back to normal. Especially since we were all moving in the right direction.

My father was due to start his trial in a few weeks. They had charged him with involuntary manslaughter and assault in the first degree. If he was to be convicted on these charges he would spend the rest of his life in jail because of his prior convictions. I had to come to the realization that I did have feelings for him. I told myself a while ago that I was going to go visit him but I never got around to it. I finally called to make a visit yesterday only to find out that I was blocked. I didn't understand. I tried to call Aunt Rosa to find out what was going on but she wasn't home. I decided to give her a try again today, this time she picked up on the second ring.

"Yes…"

"Aunt Rosa, hi, it's me…Sasha." I said nervously. This was the first time I had reached out to her since she left.

"I know who it is. What can I do for you?" she was very short with me.

"I-I wanted to make sure everything was ok with my father. I tried to make a visit and I was told he blocked me from coming to see him. I didn't understand why he would do something like that. I thought you said he wanted to see me."

Silence.

"Hello…Are you there?" I hope she didn't hang up.

I heard a heavy sigh then she spoke.

"I warned you to make things right with him over a month ago. I told you it was important that you speak to him. Now it's too late. There's nothing that can be done." She was very emotional which left me confused.

"Nothing can be done? Nothing can be done about what? I have no idea what you are insinuating."

"My heart is heavy and I feel for you. But you brought this on yourself. I love you but I can't help please don't call me anymore." Then she hung up.

I held the phone in my hand dumbfounded. I felt like I was stuck in a game of Clue. Everyone had a riddle for me to figure the hell out. Only thing is I didn't know what the hell they were talking about. I placed my cell phone on the table. I had the right mind to call her back but I know she probably wouldn't answer. Instead I grabbed my keys and badge off the refrigerator and headed down to the County. I was going to get answers one way or the other.

Chapter 28

I waited patiently in the warden's office waiting for him to give me the ok to go visit Mixxon. I was his daughter's therapist and we had a great relationship. I knew if anybody could override that block he could. The door opened and he came in.

"I have some good news for you. I have him detained in the room next door. There will be an armed guard on the outside if you need him. Take as long as you like." He said.

I shook his hand, "Thank you so much sir. I won't be long."

I walked past him and went into the next room. There was nothing but two chairs and a metal table inside. Mixxon sat at the table with his head down with shackles on both his hands and feet. For what I could see he looked as if he hadn't shaved since he got there. He had slimmed down a great deal causing him to look older than he was.

"Daddy...," I said sweetly.

He looked up at me and grunted. He had a look for repugnance on his face. I smirked. If only he knew I felt the same way too. I couldn't let him know that so I had to play nice in order to get answers.

"Look I know that you're upset with me or what have you. But Aunt Rosa said you needed to see me. So I'm here."

"I have nothing to say to you," he grumbled.

I don't know maybe I psyched myself to believe that this was going to be an easy task. My father was a stubborn man. I think that's who Azariah inherited it from.

"Please don't be that way. I would have come sooner but as you know Mom Duncan had passed and I had to get things back in order with my family." I pleaded.

"Things will never be in order. You have yourself to thank for that." He stated.

"What?"

"I should have never gotten involved with you. I should have listened to Greg you are like your mother. A conniving little bitch who thinks about no one but herself. When he told me the things he was doing to you and you allowed it to happen it made me sick. Initially I wanted to kill him but how could I blame him if you were letting it happen. It's not like he forced you. You had a choice. You are not a victim. I don't even feel sorry for what is about to come your way. You deserve it."

I just sat there with my mouth ajar. He had been talking to Greg the whole time. He knew where I was. Camille wasn't lying when she said that my father knew everything. He played me. It was fake. He didn't care about me for the last seven years everything was a fake.

"You know what you don't have to worry about what's coming my way. You need to worry about that verdict your about to receive. You're going to be locked down for the rest of your miserable life. I pray they decide to fry your ass and you go to hell with your best friend Greg." I got up from the chair and leaned over the desk until him and I were face to face.

"You're lucky it wasn't a high dosage or you could have met him sooner." I scoffed.

He smiled back at me.

I turned and walked towards the door. When I was halfway out the door.

He laughed out loud and said, "You'll see him before I will."

Chapter 28

"Happy Birthday...Mommy!" sang Lil' Jay and Azariah. They had come to my office and surprised me. Jay had walked in the door with a cake and they began to sing. Gazelle stood in the door watching the festivities with a big smile on her face. I didn't expect it because it was in the middle of a school day for one and Jay normally didn't believe in taking the kids out of school.

"Make a wish and blow out the candle Mommy" said Lil' Jay.

I took a deep breath and blew them out.

"Did you make a wish, mommy" he said. I lied and told him I did. The truth was I didn't need to make a wish everything was good in my life. Mixxon's trial was about to start, Xiomara was going to be out of my hair soon. Her and Chuck were going through a separation. Hopefully that meant she would go back to Delaware. My kids were in good health. I couldn't wish for anything else.

I noticed Azariah had drifted off in the corner. She was playing with that cellphone as usual. She was dressed in her usual posh attire. She wore a bright pink sun dress, and had her hair pulled into two nice ponytails. I thought she was a little over dressed for school.

"What are you so dressed up for?" I asked her.

She gave me a devilish grin and walked out the room. Jay and I looked at one another and shrugged our shoulders. I was happy that she was happy again.

Lil' Jay wanted me to cut the cake so he could get a piece. I really didn't want them to eat it in the office. I had a client coming in soon and didn't want my office looking a mess. I asked Gazelle to take him in the break room so he could eat it. She grabbed him and the cake and went off into the other room. That left Jay and I alone for a few minutes. I went and sat on his lap.

"Thank you so much baby." I gave him a kiss on his lips. I could feel his manhood rise under my thigh. "Uh-oh I see somebody is waking up," I said playfully.

He kissed me in my mouth deeply and began to caress my breast. I tried to pull away.

"Jay behave we can't do this," I said, but my mind and body didn't feel the same way.

"Wow thirty-nine, you better enjoy it before you get all old like me," he laughed.

I laughed with him. He was only forty-one and didn't look a day over thirty. He came closer and rubbed on my breast and whispered in my ear.

"You want to try to make another baby, before you hit the big 4-0...remember you did promise me lots of babies." He nibbled on my ear, "Lock the door." He whispered.

I got up and did it without thinking twice. By the time I turned around his pants were already at his ankles. I noticed my friend was fully erect. Matter of fact, that was the best that I had seen him in a while. Just the sight of him sent me in a frenzy. I lifted my sheath styled stress to my waistline and stepped out of my panties. I assumed position over my desk in anticipation for him to enter deeply inside me. He spread my legs and positioned me at the precise angle so he could fulfill his duties. He parted my ass cheeks and stuck his fingers deep inside. I yelped out in pain and pleasure. This was something he had never done. I didn't complain, just enjoyed it. Moments later he was stroking me like a champ I had to hold onto the desk as he went to work on me. The slapping from his balls hitting my wet pussy echoed throughout the room. I knew people heard our moans of pleasure but I didn't care. I was in bliss. He had taken me to a magical place far, far away and I didn't want to return. However I knew it was about to come to an end when he gripped on to my hips tightly and picked up his pace. I made sure that I was going to get my nut before it was too late so I started to clasp my muscles around his dick until we both came. Exhausted he lay on my back catching his breath. We both burst out laughing because we knew we were dead wrong for what we just did. But it was long overdue.

I ended up canceling my appointments and going home early. Chuck and a few of Jays friends stopped by to have a few drinks. The kids were going to stay with Sister Millie for the night. She had pretty much took Mom Duncan's place in the kids' life. It was ok because she was one of her best friends and the kids loved her. A few drinks had turned into a small pool party and a game of spades. Jay and I had reservations for the evening at this new restaurant everyone was talking about. Everyone ended up leaving around seven thirty which didn't leave me much time to get ready. Our reservations were in an hour and it was going to take us about fifteen to twenty minutes to get there. We jumped into the shower to make things go faster but that was always an issue. Back washing turned into another session which we had to cut short. I would have preferred to stay home for an all-night session but he was determined to go out.

***

We finally arrived around eight-forty; we were a little late but hopefully that wouldn't hurt anything. The restaurant was beautiful it was located in North Raleigh. There was an atrium with water features centered in the middle of the entrance. Ivory and Gold finishings were displayed throughout the area. We sat in an secluded area next to floor to ceiling windows that had a view of a colorful water display. I knew this place had to cost a fortune. The waiter came over with our menus and asked what we would be drinking. Of course Jay ordered a bottle of Ace of Spade Rosé, he could be so hood at times.

In the middle of our meal he sat his down and asked, "Are you enjoying yourself?"

"Of course I am. But you know you didn't have to spend all this money. We could have ordered out and popped some Moet and I would've been fine," I giggled; a little tipsy from the champagne.

"Seriously do you realize this is the first time I have been able to use my own money to do something for you."

It was true. I haven't touched any of the money that we got for selling the house or the business'. I had him set it up where no one other than Azariah could access the money. She wouldn't be able to touch it until she was eighteen.

I nodded my head and took a bite of my salmon.

"I have something for you." He pulled a little box from his jacket pocket and sat it in front of me. I rested my fork on my plate and opened the box. Inside was a new wedding band. It had canary yellow diamonds set in white platinum, breath taking. He took the ring from my hand and placed it on my finger.

"I want to marry you again. We need a fresh start and that's the only way things will ever get the way it should be." He was sincere.

I leaned over and kissed him passionately. Something came over me and I pulled away from him. He had a perplexed look upon his face.

"Baby...what's wrong" he asked. I was close to tears. I felt like I had a déjà vue experience. The night at Sullivan's when Lorenz proposed flashed back in my mind. That was the first time in a while that I had thought about him.

"Sasha...are you ok? He asked again.

He held my hand. I felt like I was about to hyperventilate. He got up and moved closer to me.

"I'm fine. I just-I feel sick!" I jumped up and went to the ladies room.

"Sasha are you sure you're ok? Do you need me to go with you?"

"No I'm fine. I think it may be the fish. I will be right back."

I practically ran to the restroom into the nearest stall and locked myself in. Knelt down in front of the toilet waiting for something to happen. Nothing came out but tears. I hated myself for feeling that way. What was it going to take to get over that man. I had to get myself together quickly before Jay came looking for me. I unlocked the door and grabbed some tissue and wiped my face. I realized I didn't have my purse so I couldn't put any Vizine in my eyes to clear up the redness. To my surprise they didn't have an attendant in the bathroom. I thought that to be odd. Now a days in most clubs you could fine one. You would have figured in a place like this they would have one handy.

I took a deep breath and opened the door. I felt a thud and realized I had hit someone. I began to apologize in advance.

"I am so sorry I didn't know anyone was by the door."

"Apology accepted." The voice said. The door closed and I couldn't believe my eyes.

"Greg? Is –Is that you? I blinked my eyes I had to be hallucinating or had too much to drink.

"You look stunning Sasha you have aged well." He said as he came closer. I felt his hand brush across my cheek then everything went blank.

Chapter 30

I woke up the next day in a hospital room both of my arms were strapped to the side of the bed. I looked around and noticed Jay standing by the door.

"Jay! Help me!" I tried to scream but it was more like a whisper. I felt groggy and weak. They must have drugged me or something. But why? What happened? I tried to move my arms but they didn't budge.

"Jay!" I managed to get a little louder this time he heard me and came to my side.

"Baby I'm here."

'What happened? Why am I here?"

"You don't remember?"

I shook my head no.

"Last night at dinner you went to the bathroom when you didn't come back. I went looking for you and that's when I found you passed out on the floor."

"How long have I been here and why am I in restraints?"

"You stayed the night but they had to restrain you to keep you calm. You kept screaming about he's back, he's back you never said who or what was back. You became very violent so we had to save you from hurting yourself." He said.

Then it all came back to me. I had seen Greg. I wasn't dreaming. I wanted to tell him what I had saw but I know he would think I was crazy. I didn't need any more problems. I needed to get out of there so I could protect myself and my family.

"I don't know what happened. The last thing I remembered was you saying that you wanted to marry me again then everything went blank." I lied.

He had a funny look on his face, "Are you sure?"

"Yes, I want to go home Jay. I don't want to be here anymore. Please take me home." I begged.

He gave me a kiss and rubbed the side of my face and I shuddered. That was the same thing Greg had done the night before.

"Are you sure you're ok?"

"I'm fine. I just had a chill...please get me out of here."

He went to the nurses' station and twenty minutes later I was signing myself out.

On our way home neither of us had much to say. I was trying to figure out a way to tell him what I saw so that he would believe me. Things were going so great between us. I hated to bring up the Haywards again. Especially after what we shared last night but there was no way I could deny what I saw. I know it was him. He touched me. I don't know how but he was there.

Once we were home he helped me in the house. When we were inside he hugged me tightly.

"I hate to do this particularly because of what occurred last night. I have to go out of town and handle some business. I would take you with me but the kids are in school. So I think you should go stay with my dad. I would feel much better than to leave you alone."

Here we go again. How convenient was it that out of all the times he had to go out of town now? Even though I was disappointed I didn't show it. It had been a while since he had to go out of town on business.

"I'll be fine. I just need to rest. How long will you be gone this time?"

"Just two days. I just need to tie up a few loose ends for a client."

"Ok when are you leaving? In the morning?"

"Unfortunately I have to go within the next hour. I was supposed to leave yesterday. But I couldn't miss your birthday. So I want you to rest. Sister Millie can keep the kids another night if you need her too."

I didn't want to argue so I just gave him a kiss and sent him on his way. I went upstairs and grabbed his bag and he kissed me again. I stood at the door and watched him drive off. I called Sister Millie and told her to bring my kids home. I refused to stay in that house alone. Something just wasn't right.

Chapter 31

"Azariah get up or you're going to miss the bus." I pulled the sheets of her.

She curled up in a ball, "I'm sleepy mom. I don't want to go to school." She complained.

I felt like telling her to stay home; It was my fault that she was so tired. I let them stay at Chucky Cheese last night until way after nine o'clock. I didn't feel like sitting at the house so I thought it would be good to get out for a little while. What was supposed to be an hour of dinner and play turned to over four hours. I didn't realize how hard it was to care for four children at once. I always had my sister or Aunt Rosa with me when we went out. The outing itself was a workout.

Then coming home and settling wound up children off of candy and soda was hectic. Lil' Jay decided to run all over the house while both babies wanted to cry; it was too much. By the time I got everyone settled it was after midnight. That explains why I overslept. I looked at the clock, it was after eight. There was no way she was going to get on the bus. I let her sleep a few more minutes while I showered and dressed myself. By the time I was up she was getting dressed. I threw something on the babies and Lil' Jay. They were going to daycare so it really didn't matter.

We all piled in the truck and my phone beeped. It was a text message from Jay letting me know he was about to board the plane. That made my day. We would be able to have a little quality time before the kids came home if he wasn't too tired. I dropped the kids off at daycare first before taking Azariah to school. I left her out in the car while I went in. Their teacher tried to talk me to death, I had to let her know that Azariah was late and I had to drop her off. When I came out she was knocked out asleep. I was starting to think I should just let her stay home. I didn't want her to have a bad day because she was tired. I decided against it. That would teach her a lesson about trying to stay up late. When I got to the beltway I noticed my battery light coming on. I didn't pay it any attention because we had just had the trucks serviced a few weeks ago. To be on the safe side I decided to take the back road home.

I got a good five miles and everything started to go dim and my car shut off.

"Oh my God!" I said out loud.

I drifted over to the shoulder. When I was at a complete stop I tried to unlock the doors to get out and it didn't budge.

What the fuck?

I tried the passenger door and the same thing. What is going on? Then it dawned on me I was in a BMW and when the battery dies everything locks down. I'm locked in. How is that possible? I picked up my phone to call for help and the phone battery was dead. I felt my chest tightening and I began to sweat.

"Please not now God…not now!" I was having another panic attack.

Azariah woke up,   "Mommy are you ok?" she asked calmly.

I couldn't answer her, I was too busy hyperventilating. It was like everything was closing in on me. I looked for help but no cars were coming.

Why didn't I take the highway?

"Mommy you'll be ok daddy will be here to get us soon."

"No-no daddy…doesn't know where we are." I said in between breaths.

"Yes he does he always knows where we are." She sat up in her seat and a huge smile spread on her face, "See I told you he would come!" She said pointing to the window.

An eerie feeling came over me. I turned around slowly and the devil himself was staring back at me.

***

I jumped up to the sound of my phone ringing off the hook. I picked it up but the call had ended. It was now dark outside and I was still sitting in my car.

"Zariah? Zar where are you?" I looked in the back of the truck and she wasn't there.

"Oh my God he took her I said out loud." I jumped out the truck and walked around it screaming her name. Cars began to beep at me because I had wandered onto the road. My phone rang again. I ran to the truck and answered it. It was Jay.

"Sasha where are you? It's ten o'clock at night I've been looking all over for you1"

"Jay she's gone! He took her. He took our baby Jay!" I cried.

"Sasha what are you talking about, who's gone?"

Azariah is gone. Greg took her, he took her!"

"Greg Hayward are you sure? Sasha where are you? I'm coming to get you?" he asked.

I'm on old Garner Road. Not far from the highway. Hurry I need to find my baby!"

EPILOUGUE

The Truth Shall Set You Free...

"Sasha there is so much I need to tell you. I just don't know where or how to start." Tears fell from his eyes.

We sat in the sanctuary of his father's church. Why we were here instead of a police station, I had no idea. I didn't want to hear what he had to say. I just wanted to find my child that was kidnapped by a man that was supposed to be dead.

When I initially told Jay that Greg took him he didn't seem surprised at all. But should I be surprised by it...not at all. I should have known a foundation built on deceit and lies could not withstand for long. So I listened as he purged his soul to me.

"I knew that Greg faked his death. I helped him. He told me that he just wanted to start over because he had made his life a mess. I believed him. I was going to tell you the truth after we were married but I couldn't, you see Greg knew something that would tear my family apart. He never told me exactly what it was but after you were attacked by Lorenz my father told me the truth. Camille is my sister. My father had an affair with his church secretary who happened to be Camille's mother. My mother paid Camille's mother off because if that news had gotten out, it would have ended my father's career. You know how strict they are in the South. Adultery was not tolerated. My father always sent her money and made sure she was alright. He begged me to represent her and said we were

145

her only family and it was only right. Camille promised me she would stay away if I could get her off. This year on Azariah's birthday I got a call from Greg, he wanted to see his grandchild. I told him that it wouldn't be a great idea and that's when he began to threaten me. He told me that he would tell you everything and I couldn't stand losing you."

"So Greg was stalking me after all." I couldn't believe what I was hearing.

"Yes but that's not all. I found out that Starla was secretly allowing Greg to talk to Azariah. When I found out I became angry. So I had to do something about it."

I couldn't bear to hear what he was about to say. I began to tremble.

"You killed Starla?"

"No I could never kill anyone but I hired someone to do it. I had too. She was breaking up my family. I just wanted them out of our lives, all of them. But it wasn't just me. Your father knew he was alive as well. Greg was sending him money so he could bring Azariah to see him. When I found out it was too late, she already had established a relationship with him. Then you went away on your fake business trip and did what you did and made things worse."

"How did you about the trip?"

Greg told me. He's the one who saved Camille before the entire house went up in flames. He knew everything that was going on from day one. He was pulling all the strings. I-I even knew that he was going to eventually take Azariah. That's why I became so distant towards her. I'm sorry Sasha please forgive me. Now we can start over. They have what they want they'll never come back again." He dropped to my feet and cried hysterically.

There were no words for the way I felt. I couldn't even cry. My heart was empty my mind had no thoughts. I was mentally dead. I had no idea who this man was at my feet. Nor did I know who this woman was he was crying to. Not only had I lost my first born. I had lost myself.

"Sasha please say you'll forgive me," he begged.

146

Finally the pieces where coming together. I could have prevented this if I had just told him the truth. Maybe if I would have visited my father earlier he would have let me know how much of a snake my husband was. Then there was good ol' Aunt Rosa's advice about forgiving. I looked to Jay with great pity.

"I forgive you."

"Really? Thank you Sasha!" He went to kiss me. I moved away. I wasn't finished.

"But will you be able to forgive yourself for giving away your child?" I asked calmly

"I have no claim to her. She was a Hayward and there was nothing I could do to change that." He said sadly.

"Jay my love that's where you're wrong. I retrieved my bag and pulled out the envelope that I always kept with me and handed him the papers inside."

He had a horrified look on his face. "No this can't be right! No God Please No!"

"Yes Jay. I'm sorry but it's true, you just willfully gave your firstborn to the enemy."

The End

So Real You Feel You Lived It!

Street Knowledge Publishing LLC
1902-B Maryland Ave
Wilmington, DE 19805
TOLL FREE: **1.888.401.1114**
www.streetknowledgepublishing.com

Date: _____

Purchaser _____

Mailing Address _____

City _____ State _____ Zip Code _____

Qty.	ISB Number	Title of Book	Price Each	Total
	978-0-9822515-6-0	Bloody Money	$15.00	
	978-0-9822515-9-1	Bloody Money 2	$15.00	
	978-0-9799556-4-8	Bloody Money 3	$15.00	
	978-0-9799556-0-0	Tommy Good story	$15.00	
	978-0-9822515-0-8	Tommy Good Story II	$15.00	
	978-0-9746199-1-0	Me & My Girls	$15.00	
	978-0-9746199-0-3	Cash Ave	$15.00	
	978-0-9822515-1-5	Merry F$$kin' Xmas	$15.00	
	978-0-9799556-0-7	A Day After Forever	$15.00	
	978-0-9822515-3-9	A Day After Forever 2	$15.00	
	978-0-9746199-6-5	Don't Mix the Bitter with the Sweet	$15.00	
	978-0-9799556-9-3	Playing For Keeps	$15.00	
	978-0-9799556-3-1	Pain Freak	$15.00	
	978-0-9799556-5-5	Dipped Up	$15.00	
	978-0-9799556-6-2	No Love No Pain	$15.00	
	978-0-9746199-4-1	Dopesick	$15.00	
	978-0-9799556-7-9	Lust, Love & Lies	$15.00	
	978-0-9746199-7-2	The Queen of New York	$15.00	
	978-0-9746199-8-9	Sin 4 Life	$15.00	
	978-0-9822515-4-6	A Little More Sin	$15.00	
	978-0-9746199-5-8	The Hunger	$15.00	
	978-0-9746199-3-4	Money Grip	$15.00	
	978-0-9822515-7-7	Young Rich and Dangerous	$15.00	
	978-1-944151-26-3	Street Victims	$15.00	
	978-1-944151-28-7	Street Victims II	$15.00	
	978-1-944151-30-3	Street Victimes III	$15.00	
	978-1-944151-32-4	A Small Wonder	$15.00	
	978-1-944151-45-4	Coup De Grace	$15.00	
	978-1-944151-47-8	Burton Boys (May 2017)	$15.00	
	978-1-944151-56-0	Burton Boys 2	$15.00	
	978-1-944151-58-4	Burton Boys 3	$15.00	
	978-1-944151-00-3	Dirty Living	$15.00	
	978-1-944151-65-2	Watch What You Say	$15.00	
		Total Books Ordered	Quantity	
			Subtotal	
SHIPPING/HANDLING (Via U.S. Priority Mail) $7.20 for 1st book, $2.00 for each additional book Institutional Check & Money Orders ONLY (No Personal Checks Accepted)			Shipping	
			Total	
		Total	$	

Street Knowledge Publishing LLC
1902-B Maryland Ave
Wilmington, DE 19805
TOLL FREE: **1.888.401.1114**
www.streetknowledgepublishing.com

Date: _____

Purchaser _____

Mailing Address _____

City _____ State _____ Zip Code _____

Qty.	ISB Number	Title of Book	Author	Price Each	Total
	Butterfly Collection				
		Beautiful Demise	K.D. Harris	$13.99	
		Scarred	K.D. Harris	$13.99	
		Pressure (Coming April 2017)	K.D. Harris	$13.99	
		Dying to Fit In (Coming June 2017)	K.D. Harris	$13.99	
		Legacy (Coming August 2017)	K.D. Harris	$13.99	
		Classy Clique (Coming Sept. 2017)	K.D. Harris	$13.99	
		Caged Secrets (Coming Nov. 2017)	K.D. Harris	$13.99	
		Messy Media (Coming Dec. 2017)	K.D. Harris	$13.99	
	SKP Erotica				
	978-1-944151-04-1	Beyond Measure	K.D. Harris	$15.00	
	978-1-944151-06-5	Beyond Measure II	K.D. Harris	$15.00	
	978-1-944151-62-1	Beyond Measure III (April 2017)	K.D. Harris	$15.00	
	978-1-944151-08-9	The Games We Play	K.D. Harris	$15.00	
	978-1-944151-02-7	For The Love Of It	K.D. Harris	$15.00	
	Eric B Crime Novels				
	978-1-944151-20-1	That Was Dirty	Waslim	$15.00	
	978-1-944151-22-5	It Gets Dirtier	Waslim	$15.00	
	978-1-944151-24-9	As Dirty As It Gets	Waslim	$15.00	
	978-0-9799556-8-6	Money and Murder	Fred Brown	$15.00	
	978-1-944151-35-5	Money and Murder II	Fred Brown	$15.00	
	978-1-944151-39-7	Money and Murder III	Fred Brown	$15.00	
	978-1-944151-49-2	Scandalous Ties	Jermaine "Ski" Buchanan	$15.00	
	978-1-944151-51-5	Scandalous Ties II	Jermaine "Ski" Buchanan	$15.00	
	978-1-944151-52-2	Scandalous Ties III	Jermaine "Ski" Buchanan	$15.00	
	978-1-944151-55-3	Scandalous Ties IV	Jermaine "Ski" Buchanan	$15.00	
	978-0-9799556-2-4	Courts in the Streets	Kevin Bullock	$15.00	
	978-0-9822515-5-3	Courts in the Streets II	Kevin Bullock	$15.00	
	978-1-944151-43-0	Courts in the Streets III	Kevin Bullock	$15.00	
		Total Books Ordered		Quantity	
				Subtotal	
	SHIPPING/HANDLING (Via U.S. Priority Mail) $7.20 for 1st book, $2.00 for each additional book Institutional Check & Money Orders ONLY (No Personal Checks Accepted)			Shipping	
				Total	
		Total		**$**	

149

www.ingramcontent.com/pod-product-compliance
Lightning Source LLC
Chambersburg PA
CBHW031454260626
47154CB00017B/2808

9 781944 151065